fic
Bie

Copy 2
6076

DATE DUE

JAN 2 3			
MAY 1 7			
APR 1 7			
OCT 2 0 1997			
NOV 0 3 1997			

fic
Bie

6076

Copy 2

Biemiller, Carl L.
The hydronauts

B 35-157

THE HYDRONAUTS

THE
HYDRONAUTS

Carl L. Biemiller

Doubleday & Company, Inc.   Garden City, New York

Library of Congress Catalog Card Number 70–97651
Copyright © 1970 by Carl L. Biemiller
All Rights Reserved
Printed in the United States of America

Book One
THE KELP FOREST

The range was not the entire world. But it was more than eighty percent of it, and all water. The nuclear war had long since melted much of the polar ice caps. Whole sections of continents were long gone. The range was life. It supplied many of the raw materials of civilization for the hive cities. Those cities lay burrowed deep in North and South America, Asia, Africa, Europe, and Australia. Where England had been was part of the open range. And the range was a global warehouse which also stored man's equipment for survival.

Kim Rockwell, Marine Warden Third Class, was working a small portion of it, and that was not pleasant at the moment. But it was better than being in the cities. He was lucky to be in the sea at all. And even the brightest of Wardens III do not get fancy range jobs. Not when they are seventeen. He could take some pride in himself, however. The International Marine Council screened only the best of the youth candidates chosen by the Career Boards for Underwater Cadet and Warden Training.

He had worked hard ever since he left the Municipal Nursery where all children were graded for future places in society. He had studied the science of the sea eight hours a day for more than ten years. And he even had studied at night when the hypnosleep machines turned his dreams into classrooms to add more knowledge.

Kim was aware that he would never live long enough to know enough, which is remarkable *enough* for seventeen.

The seas had also changed in the two centuries since the man-made suns seared earth with radioactive death. The old knowledge of oceans and ocean life was still on the library shelves, the microfilms, the tape records buried before the war. But the life forms within the depths, even the character of some waters themselves, had altered during the trial of heat and radiation. Winds, waves, and currents were different than those recorded in the past. And there were Wardens of Commander Grade who argued that the rotation of the earth, and maybe its orbit around the sun too, had altered.

Kim was cruising the kelp forest. It was spooky today. The sky, some one hundred and fifty feet above at the sea surface, was overcast and dull gray. But even on the brightest days the forest was dark and moody, its light dimmed by the giant, floating fronds of the huge algae and the thicketlike stipes of stems of the ancient crop. The water was full of bouncing spores. They pinged off his itchy gill suit.

The silco-membrane suit was not only skintight. It was quite literally skin, with an inner lining of pore-penetrating follicles of hairs. They reached beneath Kim's own tawny hide to his blood stream to supply him with oxygen directly from the water and to remove the carbon dioxide from his system at the same time. Kim's lungs were working on exercise alone. He was breathing like a fish. But the gill suit itched. The darkness and the hailstorm of spores annoyed him.

He kicked his swim fins and glided, trying to decide whether the gathering darkness made the light from the equipment pack on his chest necessary. That keel-shaped pack held so much junk he almost hated to open it—working tools, communications devices, lunch pellets, a small drug-gun powerful enough to paralyze the motor muscles and nerves of all but the largest of the sea predators likely to appear in the forest.

There had been a forest of kelp, giant algae, along the southern California coast of North America for centuries. Men had harvested it since the nineteenth century, mostly for food and drugs. But in the generations since the nuclear war, the changed sea had altered the forest. Its plants grew to weird immensities with stipes, or stems, as thick as ancient earth tree trunks and with fronds and leaves as large as great floating tents.

Men still harvested the kelp for the substance called algin which made a gluelike jelly that both preserved food shipped from the sea and made containers for it which, like rubbery missiles, could be shot through the compressed air, food-freight tubes to the cities inland. More important, men mined the forest.

The great plants absorbed vast amounts of minerals through their fronds: cobalt, iron, nickel, lead, tin, zinc. The minerals obtained after processing were reasonably pure too. They were not like the crazy, unstable, radioactive isotopes from the mines of land. And they were vital to man.

It was Kim's job and the work of many other wardens to make the kelp flourish, to record its progress, to aid in its harvest. He worked by day as the plants did, using their chlorophyll and sunlight energy to grow and to store their minerals.

At night he slept in a pressurized silicate bubble anchored eighty feet down on the bottom. He breathed compressed air from the bubble's own units or fresh air valved in from a snorkel tube fastened to a tank buoy, which also marked the bubble's location on the sea surface. It was home, where he could peel off the gill suit and rub algin lotion on his skin to remove the day's tickles. The bubble was hot shower baths, hot meals, and a bed. It was an office where sonar devices pinged and radar and TV spied on his sector of the forest. It was a toy laboratory, a place where temperature charts were kept, salinity and sea chemical tests recorded. It was his house three months out of four. The fourth was a leave month, usually spent in the onshore headquarters compound miles south in Baja California.

He shared the bubble with his patrol buddy, cocustodian of Sector 12 Forest Area 80, the five square miles of their joint responsibility.

Her name was Toby Lee. She was a year older than Kim, but he ranked her by one month in the same grade, Warden Third Class. He had the uneasy feeling that she knew more about the work than he did, however. She came from a long line of fishery and sea-farm experts.

She was Japanese. If the history books were right, the nation of her ancestors, now only a single tiny island, had been taking ninety percent of its proteins from the sea for a thousand years. She was a hard worker. She was a fun person. And she was doll high with a face like a flower and an all-girl form.

Not that *that* mattered. The International Marine council was resolute in the manner in which it conditioned members of the Warden Service for life in the sea. Toby's shape was merely feminine.

Right now it was missing, and the forest gloom was deepening.

By normal routine she shouldn't be too far away, but it was easy enough to remain unseen in the kelp lanes. More sea life than man ever knew about had hidden in the beds or taken refuge from predators there from time immemorial. And she might be doing a hundred things that evening like taking core samples from the stipes for mineral content analysis.

Kim picked up the warbler snapped to the top of his chest pack and spoke into it. The sound waves pulsed far and fast through the water.

"Toby. Come in, Toby. Time to knock off, time to swim home."

The receiving units on the rim of his goggle mask trilled faintly.

"Whose home?" they chittered in soprano sonics.

Twelve feet of bottle-nose tursiops, a dolphin weighing half a ton, slipped between kelp stipes and grinned at him.

"If there's anything I hate it's a big joker," said Kim
through the warbler. "I'm worried, Pudge. I can't raise
Toby. She ought to be working within a few hundred
yards of here at this time of day. We're not far from the
bubble. Want to take a look for me?"

The sleek mammal slipped out of sight with one surge
of fluked tail. The sound in Kim's mask receivers whined
up the auditory range beyond his hearing as the dolphin
beamed on its own echo-location mechanism.

For the millionth time as he swam in its general wake,
Kim appreciated the aquatic miracle that was the dolphin
and the intelligence long inherent in its brain capacity—
always physically larger than man's. Communication with
it, perfected originally with sonic codes, had evolved
through years of in-sea teamwork into something near
direct mental contact, a direct exchange of thoughts.

The pelagic, "open sea range" herds, which supplied
meat and leather to the burrow cities of the wasted continents, could not be handled without dolphin help. The
bay area food shark complexes, even estuarial sea farms,
could not be efficient without their assistance. Without
their affection and friendship, the subsea continental
shelves and deep slopes, even the sea surfaces, would
destroy men with loneliness, if not with other perils.

Pudge and an equally sizable female named Peggy
worked this sector with Kim and Toby although they
were on call for many duties when needed anywhere.
Mostly they spent their time urging grazing fishes through
the sound barrier lanes resonated through the forest. They
chased kelp perches, foot-long anchovies, and overgrown

sardines south so they didn't have time to chew the mineral-laden fronds into shreds. They carried special equipment and messages from the camp bubbles between the sectors of forest which stretched some two hundred miles along the coast. They were watchdogs as well as guardians against many marauders, sharks, giant squids, rays. They were invaluable detectors of changes in the sea which sometimes escaped the sensing equipment of man.

But where was Toby?

Kim's receivers vibrated.

"Trouble," reported Pudge. "Found her but she's unconscious. Am taking her to bubble. Meet us there. Don't try to join us here. Poison water!"

Kim picked up a darker thought from the dolphin.

He swam, every muscle in his young athlete's body straining as alarm gave him extra strength. He wished he had taken one of the water ejection jet sleds on patrol that morning. He steadied his thinking.

"Can you give me an idea of her condition?" he warbled. "Any apparent suit rips or wounds?" Already warden discipline and warden training had freed his mind for emergency action.

"Think drowned," was the answer. "Water this area stained odd brown similar to blood. No suit rips. No wounds."

In Kim's mind there was a clear, if fleeting, picture of this patient cetacean, his gentle teeth holding Toby's underarm and shoulder firmly, moving swiftly toward the bubble with Toby's slim body streamed to the dolphin's dark sides. His mind grew cold and busy.

"How's your own air?" he piped. Then, before the answer, he said, "Leave her at the bubble. When you surface to blow see if the stain goes all the way to the surface and check the wave action up there, the wind too."

Without losing a stroke he reached into his chest pack for the compact, fist-sized communicator and began his report to base. It was a report that would be picked up and recorded by every picket bubble in the forest as well as the headquarter compound in Baja. If one would advance in the Service, every sea condition, every emergency, anything both usual and unusual, were ultimately transmitted to base, some things merely faster than others. Kim wanted to advance. He had been taught that way.

He had not been taught to block out the sickening, frightening thought that Toby might not be alive, not alive, not alive this moment.

He found her half lifted into the open water hatch leading into the bottom level of the bubble where Pudge had placed her. In one swoop he was over her, hoisting her into breathable air on the grilled deck below the living area. He stripped the gill suit from her quickly and lifted her gently through the hatch to the main bubble floor.

Her honey-colored body was cold and faintly tinged with a purple cast. She was not breathing. He found a medical blanket, set it to full heat, and wrapped her slight form within it. Without taking time to remove his own gill suit, he threw his mask off, gulped deeply and began mouth-to-mouth, artificial respiration, not yet wishing to use the high oxygen drug injection directly into the blood stream until the lungs were partially active. He worked patiently, remembering all the instructors who said, "There is either all the time you need or never enough, and no limit on either."

He remembered other tips. "Make sure you lift the chest cavity. Check for water in the lungs. It is carbon dioxide in the blood which causes the brain to 'tell' the body to breathe." Little scraps of thought jumbled in his head.

He worked steadily, patiently, with a paced rhythm as the minutes passed.

Others too worked. Back at Baja, headquarter wardens passed quiet orders along the bubble network. Men from the next nearest Forest Area in Sector 12 took tool-laden water jet sleds and left their patrol range for Kim's. A picket hovercraft, riding herd on the whale range some fifty miles east of the kelp belt, streaked off post, picked up a doctor from a mother ship, and whizzed for Kim's marker buoy.

Commander Tod Torrance spoke quietly to his assistant at Baja. "Is this Rockwell youngster steady?" he asked.

"Good cadet record," replied his coworker. "But this is his first solo emergency outside of two brushes with sharks. And you'll notice his report was detailed even if he must have been in a tearing hurry to reach Lee. I don't like that stained water. It must be taking dissolved oxygen out of the sea at a big rate. If it caught and suffocated

Lee without much warning, it could destroy a lot of kelp too. Want to raise Rockwell directly?"

Commander Torrance was a spare man with some thirty years in the Service. It had been a long time since he had personally served on in-sea duty, but he remembered every single thing he had ever learned beneath the surface. He rubbed a hand over his gray head thoughtfully.

"He'll be working on Lee," he said. "And he'll be beginning to have big doubts. Raise him by voice, but don't ask for a report, just encourage him. I'm wondering if Lee didn't get a big intake of some toxic, a direct poison instead of the drowning process that Rockwell is treating. But call now."

Assistant Commander Jiggs Jensen, nearly as long in the Service as Torrance, nodded gravely. He was a big man, but his voice was surprisingly gentle as it drifted into Kim's bubble from the instrument console speakers.

"Don't bother answering," it said. "There's a doctor on the way for Toby Lee and two men from Area 81 to help. Don't give up on Lee. And don't think about water condition in your sector. You're doing fine. Over for now."

The two veteran wardens looked at each other. On in-sea duty, men needed what support they could get. Their glances mirrored surprise and sudden alertness. The speaker in the Baja office went into action. The voice coming from it was strained but firm.

"Sir, I have given up on Lee as a drowned person. I have been thinking of water condition. Five minutes ago I treated Lee for poison. I think she may have taken it into her blood stream through the gill suit, and that it came from toxic plankton. I gave her adrenalin from the first-aid supplies. I injected it into the nearest artery to her heart that I could find. I hope it was the right decision. . . ."

Kim's voice from the bubble faltered. It shook a little.

Commander Torrance reached for the speaking unit and spoke calmly. "Good boy, Rockwell," he said. "The doctor should be with you any minute. The decision seems correct. I suggest you keep up the chest massage. I further suggest that you place Toby Lee on a bunk bed and tie her there as firmly as possible. Repeat. Tie her into the bunk. She may regain consciousness violently. Repeat. Tie her. If your judgment is sound, she could shake herself into heart failure. Report as you will."

"Well, we know he thinks and has courage enough to act," said Assistant Commander Jensen. "I'll raise that picket hovercraft and alert the doctor. It might save him some time."

Kim never knew just when he had begun to concentrate on the fact that Toby's trouble might not be caused by a lack of oxygen, that the dolphin's thought about drowning might not be right. He knew that Toby was not responding to artificial respiration. And she should have been. He didn't know how long he had been working on her when the thought of poison—as poison, that is—passed through his mind. Had he wasted too much time? Too much precious time?

Poison water, the dolphin had reported. The intelligent mammal was never wrong about changes in the sea. But what kind of poison? What kind of natural taint in this section of the Pacific coastline? He kept right on working, forcing air into Toby's lungs, but he searched his mind back through old lessons, old studies, as he worked.

The sea was full of life forms, many that could only be detected and studied through a microscope. They were the drifters called plankters. They were plant planktons and animal planktons. They were food for other tiny forms of life. Indeed, some of them were food for the largest animals and fishes in the sea, some types of whales, for instance. Among them, these primitive organisms too small to see with the naked eye, these things called phytoplanktons, were certain forms called dinoflagellates. These microscopic organisms had characteristics of both plants and animals.

They had another characteristic too, Kim remembered suddenly. Sometimes they multiplied. They flowered and turned poisonous. The flowering, according to the old books, caused "red tides." Then marine creatures, tidewater fish, crabs, mussels, rays, eels, and others died by the millions.

Pudge had reported that the sea around Toby was stained brown, like old blood. Could Toby have taken in dinoflagellate poison through the gill suit? If so, it would have blocked her heart action, frozen her muscle action.

He made his decision. He acted upon it. He left Toby and stumbled to the well-stocked medical kit, half wondering why he still had swim fins on his feet. He found the hypo needle, sought among the carefully labeled stimulants for the ampoule marked adrenalin. He fixed the hypo and made the injection. His fingers trembled slightly on Toby's satin skin, warm from the blanket. They were still trembling when Assistant Commander Jensen's voice reached into the bubble. He felt very old, very tired. But he made his report as soon as the comfort of Jensen's message settled about him. And he snapped to a wary attention at Commander Torrance's instructions.

Kim left Toby in the blanket as he placed her on her bunk. He bound her firmly with two sections of filament netting sometimes used for taking small fishes from the kelp fronds for study. He settled beside her on his knees, and awkwardly but effectively, he applied pressure and release to her rib cage.

He knew about in-sea dangers. Long instruction, long training had given him a built-in awareness of the death that lives in many forms in the sea range. This, if it came to Toby, was his own death too, as she had become part of his daily being. He waited and grew up beside her as young soldiers once grew up in combat during all of man's wars but the last one.

Then her chest fluttered. He could feel her tremble. He bent his mouth to hers and began again the respiratory process. He felt her shake as though something inside her was trying to get out. Her eyes opened and looked through him into nothing. They saw him and knew him.

The communications console spoke.

"This is Doctor Felipe Baguio. We're right above you. Sea is calm. Wind no force at all. We're lowering a pressure capsule to your bottom hatch. The dolphin is steadying the cable to you. I'm coming down on a weighted dive. Give me a reading on your bubble pressure so I can stabilize the capsule for the patient."

Kim gave him the figures automatically.

"It's dark up here so I'll be a few minutes," said Dr. Baguio. Kim had not noticed the cold light come on from the silicate bubble walls as it did automatically each day when the surface above met nightfall. The people from Area 81 must be coming in on laser light units to cut the muck outside.

There was color flooding Toby's face, and her lips were moving. His feeling moved up in his throat and choked him, and he swallowed.

There was noise from the sea hatch deck below. He left Toby and looked down. The doctor, his wet suit dripping, was slipping out of a small tank harness and dropping a weight belt, which fell with a chunk.

He was a small, wiry man with a pug-nosed, bland, brown face. Even motionless for the moment, he looked very busy. "I heard from Base on the way," he said. "Let's see the patient. Capsule is down. You've got other visitors too. A couple of men attaching sleds, and a nosy dolphin who sends his regards. Come on now."

Dr. Baguio was deft and sure as he examined Toby Lee. He talked to himself as much as he talked to Kim. "Toxic all right. Poison right to the entire motor system. Some kind of an alkaloid with a nitrogen base. There's an antidote for something like this in your kit made right from your garden of kelp. But how would you know? Stimulant was right too, but there's a better one in the kit

too. How would you know? She's a hospital job. Have to watch brain damage."

He straightened and look directly into Kim's miserable eyes.

"You did fine, son," he said.

"Will she be all right?" asked Kim.

"Think so now. Don't really know. As soon as I do, you'll know."

With the two men from Area 81 helping, they placed a drowsing Toby into the capsule and sealed her there. The capsule was really a self-contained depth-metal pod. It maintained its own inner pressure set at whatever depths from which its occupant had been rescued. It supplied its own oxygen mixes, its own heat. It could be set to provide massage for circulation, even give anti-pain or food injections. Although such capsules were usually lowered by cable for exact position placement, they had their own buoyancy attachments and could pop directly to the surface for immediate pickup. This one would attach to the flat hull of the picket hovercraft and be zoomed to the base hospital at Baja within minutes.

"So long," said the little doctor cheerfully. "Glad there wasn't anything messy down here like shark attack. Make your own report to headquarters, Rockwell. I'll make mine on the way. Suggest you use shield suits and air tanks if you're going to work bad water. Gill suits would put the stuff right into your blood stream. I'm off."

He slipped into his gear, pushed through the lower hatch and vanished.

A big part of Kim had already gone before the doctor,

with Toby. But the first duty of the Service is the Service. He turned to face the wardens from Area 81 who were watching him. They introduced themselves. Although their names were familiar to Kim, their persons were not, only their voices. Changing shifts, different duty hours, varied leave times did not make for many close acquaintances within Forest Sectors. But the bond of common work, shared danger, and the dependence of each upon another made them closer than the families in the old history books once were.

Tuktu Barnes was wide and stocky with a deep chest and a vast spread of shoulder muscles. His face was flat and looked flatter as he grinned in a huge smile. He came from the North, from the McKinley City deep within the Alaskan mountain ranges, and had taken his training there. He had served a brief apprenticeship in the Bering Sea before his transfer to the Kelp Forest. Many generations ago Tuktu's ancestors had been Eskimos. He was a specialist, or going to be, in nutrients, the foods of the plants, mammals and fishes, the foods of mollusks. He would someday help man enrich the many "desert" areas of the range—as an old-time farmer used fertilizers—to support useful life which would, in turn, support the cities.

Genright Selsor, who was Tuktu's patrol buddy, was slender and somehow angular. He was relaxed, genial, and black as the night within the abysses of the sea. He had been schooled in the great burrow city that lay safe and busy under the plateau of ancient Ethiopia. He too had served a short apprenticeship in-sea off the coast of southwest Africa before transfer. The Service did move its

people, as it would move Kim. Selsor hoped, someday, to be one of the great oceanographic chemists.

Both Tuktu and Genright were Wardens III. Each ranked Kim by nearly a year. Each was older. Tuktu was eighteen, Genright nineteen. As members of ancient armies once did, each had made a point of rank with their introductions.

Kim was not impressed. The accident to Toby, whether he knew it or not, had already given him a new firmness. And this was his area, Area 80, not 81. He was careful in his conduct, however.

"I've got to report to Base," he said. "I'm responsible here, responsible for the whole area with Lee gone, unless otherwise instructed. Here's what I now know. . . ."

He told them of the dolphin's findings of poison water. He gave details of Toby's condition and his action. He filled them in on the doctor's opinion, added his own ideas about dinoflagellates. He told them of the doctor's report of surface calm and lack of surface winds.

"Anything either of you can add from your own trip from your bubble to this one?"

Tuktu and Genright accepted Kim's leadership calmly. Tuktu spoke. "We came fast and more prepared to give you physical help if you and Lee needed it than anything else. Base had told us about the poison water so we came in shield suits, using tanks with all the junk we could find on the sleds."

Genright interrupted. "I don't think we came through the danger area. We might not have noticed anyhow. It was dark and visibility in the whole forest isn't too good under the best of conditions. I did notice a definite set of current which bends toward the coast. It may be moving the tainted water east and north from here if there is no wind and wave action at work. I think Tuktu might agree also that we didn't notice any water disturbance, any turbulence. One other thing. I think we crossed one of your fish lanes. We picked up some slow traffic moving south in our laser light tubes, but no dead fish."

"But if that stuff is robbing plants of oxygen we could lose a lot of kelp, mused Tuktu. "Anyhow," he added, "I'm not about to go out and roam until we can see."

"Think there's any chance that there could be any gunk in the poison zone which would show?" asked Kim thoughtfully.

"It's your house," said Tuktu.

Kim nodded. He moved to the instrument console, adjusted the radar controls and began a 360-degree sweep. His visitors peeked at the screen with him. Kelp stipes. Moving blips in the north-south fish lanes. A boat-sized blip near the surface.

"Oh, boy," said Tuktu.

"Shark, probably a big blue," murmured Genright.

A smudge, but bright, trailing light on the screen.

"Squid," said Kim, "big one, and dragging three-quarters of himself behind him. They come four tons out of Monterey Bay once in a while, and they can eat twelve hundred pounds of marlin for a snack."

There were two blips, fair sized, almost motionless directly above the bubble and only about three feet from the surface of the sea.

"I know them," drawled Genright. "Pudge and Peggy. Some work. Others sleep. But they sure are good to Tuktu and me."

Kim made a slight control change. There was a straight line of light, broken with an indentation, and in front of it, fanning into the darkness, was a pale blur, a phantom of cloud.

"That's shore line," he said, "and something coming from it into the sea which fades away. Take a good look, Selsor. You want to be a chemist. Is that a chemical cloud or a physical one?"

"Whatever it is, it's an active radar wave conductor," said Genright.

"Of course," snapped Kim, "of course, of course . . ."

He snapped open the communicator to Baja headquarters, using the bubble network channel so the whole forest could hear. "Rockwell reporting to Base," he said, "as ordered."

"And some later than expected," muttered Assistant Commander Jensen to Commander Torrance, both still on duty. "All right, Rockwell, let's hear it," he said firmly.

Kim took a deep breath. "You will have had the doctor's report, sir," he said.

"Too true," mouthed Jensen.

"Barnes and Selsor are with me. I am not taking them out until first light."

"Something else we know about Rockwell," murmured Jensen, "They outrank him, but he's taken over on his own base."

"They did not encounter bad water to the best of their

knowledge enroute. They report firm current set which, in the absence of wave and wind action, suggests to them that poison may be moving north and east. I agree from my personal knowledge of the area."

"Do you now," said Commander Torrance softly.

"Suggest, sir, that all forest bubbles make a scan of the coastline at intersect Coordinates Forty and One-eighty South, and if base thinks justified that some overflight be made in the area. The scope here picked up sort of a cloud showing, sir. It might indicate something flowing from land to sea which might have changed the water elements, maybe causing a poison area. This is only an idea, sir."

Kim paused. "Has there been any overland rain in that region?"

At Baja, Commander Torrance looked at Jensen, then spoke into the communicator. "That's desert, Rockwell. It has been for a hundred years. What are you suggesting? Some rainwater runoff carrying radioactivity from an old war pocket that would affect plankton?"

"Yes, sir," said Kim simply.

"We'll check," said the commander. "Meanwhile, all bubbles make scan and report. Rockwell, Barnes, and Selsor, we'll get additional men into your present area as needed. But I expect a complete check from you as soon as possible. You'll be glad to know that Lee is responding to care. One more thing, have you checked all water temperature reading stations on the master bubble chart of your area?"

"Oh, golly, sir," said Kim.

"Out," said Baja Base to the network.

"One other thing we know about Rockwell," said the commander to his assistant. "He gets ideas and isn't afraid to state them. He also goofs but he doesn't apologize about it."

Commander Torrance was wrong. Back in Bubble 80 Kim grimaced at Tuktu and Genright. "How dumb can I get? I was even too dumb to say I was sorry."

"We agree," said Tuktu. "You almost had us thinking you were bright. If I don't catch some sleep, I'll be dumber than you are."

Kim grinned. "Okay," he said, "I'll give them the readings, as if they didn't already have them back at base. Sack out. I'll be right behind you."

There was only one light in the forest in the morning. It was comprised of different degrees of shadow. It was almost always dark under the canopy of kelp fronds, which hid millions of the smaller fish from the greater ones which preyed upon them. Sometimes there seemed to be more light near the bottom where moray eels, rock fishes, brittle stars, abalones, and lobsters watched an endless parade of life from their own hidey holes. Even the huge holdfasts, root structures, of the kelp stipes teemed with life, most of them microscopic in size, some of them dangerous to the valuable kelp crop.

Kim noticed that the sea urchins were getting out of hand again despite constant efforts to get rid of them. Urchins, those walking pincushions of living spines, ate the

key, or primary, stipe of a plant leaving it to float free
and die.

He thought about bringing the sea otter packs back for
a week or so. The sea otters, tame and joyful beasts whose
gleaming pelts once caused wars in long-past centuries,
loved urchins. They loved them for breakfast, lunch, and
dinner. The otter herdsmen moved them about the forest
from time to time to grow fat while controlling pests.

The forest was a jungle all right. It was a nursery and
a slaughterhouse too where wandering giants of the sea
often cruised seeking easy food.

It felt restless that morning. He didn't know about
Tuktu or Genright, but Kim felt a vast unease, an itch of
trouble. For no definite reason, he felt wary, extra alert.

They had not yet found tainted water although the
dolphins were making wide-ranging casts. And they
too were moving with some speed using sleds, stopping
only to take water samples and to examine darker sections of the forest for dead fish. They checked the clusters
of tiny life forms which attached themselves to kelp
fronds and filtered their food from the water. They would
die first from poison.

There was normal movement in the fish lanes, the traffic of grazing fish which had to be kept from the kelp as
much as possible, and bigger fish pursuing the grazers.
All of them, however, were impelled by their own sensory urges through the lanes.

The lanes were two parallel lines of small nuclear
power packs spaced at intervals some three hundred feet
apart. The distance between the lines was about one hun-

dred yards, the "highway" down which the fish swam. The packs emitted sound waves geared to an unpleasant frequency which formed, in a sense, a barrier on either side of the "highway." Since everything in the sea is, in some measure, sensitive to sonic impulses which guide much of fish movement, the fish stayed in the "middle of the street." They moved rapidly when chased either by the dolphins or other creatures seeking snacks. The packs served another purpose. They could be controlled also to produce heat which caused thermal, or heat, currents to rise from the sea floor. Thus the rich food, or nutrients, in the sediments of the bottom rose to feed plankton which in turn fed the fish which ate plankton.

Plankton eaters, like herring, sardines, and anchovies, swimming down the "highway," literally swam in a never-ending chain of roadside restaurants.

"I think we ought to check in with base," suggested Kim through the warbler. "Anybody think otherwise?"

"Are we almost out of your area?" asked Tuktu.

"Nearly," answered Kim. "Genright, you're the chemist, do you think the stuff's dispersed or diluted so much we can't find it? Or what's your guess about current moving it out to sea away from the forest?"

"Could be either," warbled Genright. "Might also be that if it were flagellates carrying the stuff that they too died of it, and whatever it was is now part of some sediment on the bottom somewhere."

"But if Kim's guess that the infection was coming from land was right, there ought to be more bad water moving our way," said Tuktu.

"Unless base somehow stopped the flow," added Genright.

"Or unless it was just one bad, hot pocket that got flushed out by rain back on the land, and that was the end of it," warbled Kim. "I'm going to call in the dolphins before I report." He felt somehow sick to think that Toby might have been trapped in just a freak patch of ocean and nearly died. He had another thought, a strange one. Could people still die in a war two hundred years old? Of course they could. The earth was sick. Otherwise the cities would not hide so deep within it.

Pudge and Peggy arrived in a boil of water from their own speed. Pudge wore a crown of kelp stipes that he had torn off in passage. He looked like a grin wearing a wig, and he nuzzled and bumped Kim into a slow somersault, almost shifting the compact tank from his shield suit. He was glad to see him. He always was. He didn't need code or trills to say so. Kim could feel the cetacean's thought, and he sensed that Tuktu could also. Tuktu might have told him that a couple of million years' worth of Eskimos had talked to fish, whales, seals, foxes, and a lot of other wild things as well.

If Pudge looked silly, Peggy was ridiculous. She was a bigger creature than the male dolphin, maybe fifteen feet in length and thicker through the girth. She had slammed through something that left a dab of phosphorescent slime on her dorsal fin and around her mouth. Her grin was green and it glowed. Her dorsal fin looked like some strange plant growing from her spine. She too nuzzled Kim and spun him into a slow turn.

"Report, report, you lumps," snapped Kim. "Did you find bad water? Did you see dead fish? What about the sea?"

The dolphins had ranged far, into and past the areas adjacent to Kim's own. The surface sea was quiet, winds gentle. There was no bad water that they had found. There were no dead fish except some they had eaten. A killer whale of great size had skirted the seaside of the forest, swimming fast to the south. They had given it room and hidden even if the killer whale was their own first cousin. There were boats in the sky headed for the area. That was all. Yet, added Pudge, to him the entire range along the coast seemed alert and waiting for something.

"Let's check in to base," said Genright.

Kim snapped on the communicator. "Rockwell here, and Barnes and Selsor, Area 80 Patrol . . ."

"Come in, Rockwell, we've been expecting you. This is Lieutenant Rang."

"We have found no poison water, sir," said Kim. "Dolphins have covered two areas beyond us to the north and indicate no altered sea. Forest seems normal, sir. But dolphins reported surface craft approaching this vicinity."

He paused. One did not ask questions in the Service. The lieutenant would tell him what he saw fit to tell him.

Genright asked the lieutenant for him.

"Any findings at base, sir, about cause of tainted water?"

Their receivers chuckled.

"Rockwell," said the lieutenant from Baja, "Commander

Torrance asked me to tell you that the weather people
claim not a drop of rain has fallen at Coordinates Forty
and One-eighty South for fifty years."

An edge of silence sliced off conversation. The lieutenant continued. "He and investigation crew were into the
coast early, however. He asked me to tell you that it is
better to be lucky than right. They found remains of
an old atomic desalinization plant from the days when
they first made fresh water from salt. The walls which
held the old coolant system for the pile had burst from
age. What liquid was left ran off over a hard-baked surface into the sea. There wasn't too much of it apparently,
but it poisoned a small area of the sea with radioactive
plankton. The commander thought dinoflagellates too.
He commended you."

"Thank you, sir," said Kim.

"Don't interrupt, Warden Three. The dolphin report of
craft in your vicinity is correct. It is early in the season,
but rather than risk the slightest danger to the kelp, the
commander has ordered harvest crews to cut crop. Barnes
and Selsor will return with you to bubble where you will
all stand by to assist at Harvest Master's orders. That is
all for now."

"Well," warbled Tuktu, "we'd have had to come over
and help cut hay anyhow."

They pointed the sleds for Bubble 80, moved through
the patrol alleys in the gently waving, swaying, dancing
stipes.

As they towed behind the jet sleds, Kim wondered
about his edginess. The forest still didn't feel right. Was

it because there might still be a patch of poison water wandering among the kelp?

He had heard old instructors talk about "sea feel" and how the best of wardens seemed to have it as an extra instinct. He was too new in the Service to talk about such matters, but yet he knew that the way one grew wise in the sea was to use every sense possible, even at the risk of seeming foolish to others.

He thought about the harvest craft above. They were flat bargelike boats equipped to travel as hovercraft or to float on the sea surface. Booms extended from their sides to tow-cutting vanes, set for varying depths, which pruned through the dark algae like old-fashioned lawn mowers or grain harvesters used on land farms before the world went underground. Sometimes the cables of the cutting vanes tangled in heavy kelp, and then the wardens worked to free them. And that was hard, awkward work.

When the harvest floated free, the cutting vanes were stowed away, and great grabs of what looked like woven metal baskets were lowered from the booms to pluck the kelp from the surface and dump it into the barges on its first step to the processing factories.

A mother ship accompanied the harvest fleet as a dormitory for the harvest crews, a communications center, and an emergency hospital. The mother ship monitored the entire area during operations as did the headquarters base at Baja.

If things went right, several sections of the forest could be cut and loaded upon the barges in a few days.

But occasionally things did not go right. Nobody was

ever sure, despite the constant patrols from the area bubbles on the sea bottom, just what the harvesting might stir from the kelp or what sort of creatures the activity might attract to the area.

Kim realized this. So did Tuktu and Genright.

"Let's move a bit nearer bottom," suggested Kim. "Might make a little better time. These shield suits and tanks slow us some despite the sleds. And I think we could use some lights. Okay?"

"Good idea," warbled Genright.

"Maybe," added Tuktu, "but swimming is easier than chopping grass, and you know what they'll want us for when we get back."

Kim hesitated. "This may sound silly," he said, "but it will only take a second. I want something a bit bigger than a hand light. Let me get the laser from the sled, and I just might grab a drug-gun too."

"Jumpy?" asked Genright.

"Some," said Kim evenly.

"Me too," said Tuktu suddenly.

They rummaged with equipment clips on the sleds, and went on, spraying radiance through the lanes. Some sizable abalones swam by ejecting water from their shells, which they clapped like hands for motion. The sudden light had them looking for darkness. Green and red sea anemones, more like bloated flowers than living creatures, flexed nervously on the bottom.

Tuktu saw it first. His warbler squeaked. Kim automatically set his communicator to full send and receive. Genright named it.

"Giant squid!"

A single press of a stud on the rodlike laser light he carried made it both a light and a tight-beam heat ray capable of boring a hole through rock.

Even as he pressed it, Kim automatically recalled what he knew about the monster looming ahead. The cephalopods, the class of mollusks, including squids, octopuses, and cuttlefishes. Meat eaters, and lightning fast in the water. Destroyers of man, fish, able to do battle with whales. Even before the war there were species sixty feet long, two tentacles, eight arms, monstrous mouths, huge eyes of perfect vision. Even hundreds of years before the war, there were myths of the kraken, the squid which demolished whole fishing boats.

"Tuktu! Genright! Split!" he commanded. "Separate!" He spoke into his communicator. "Giant squid," he reported. "Suggest any surface craft lift from water."

There was a hiss and a boil of tiny bubbles as Kim's laser beam lanced ahead into what seemed a wall of great grasping arms and tentacles.

Tuktu's sled peeled off to the right, banging against kelp stipes. Genright's turned left down a fish lane. Kim angled his toward the surface in an effort to rise above the monster.

He heard Tuktu's voice burble like flute music.

"This thing's forever," it said. "It must be a hundred yards long!"

Kim kept his thumb on the firing stud as he angled upward, trying for the great squid's eye. A coil of rubbery arm, round as a barrel, tipped his sled and sent it spinning away from him. He held hard to the laser and dived for the bottom. The arm drew the entire sled into a writhing nest of flesh. Kim swam desperately for one of the huge, igloolike holdfasts which anchored the kelp plants.

From the corner of his eye he saw a blinding streak of light, then another. Tuktu and Genright, from somewhere down the length of the monster, were firing into the bulk.

There was a smother of bubbles and a heaving swell of water as if the ocean were suffering some internal storm. There was a brittle crackling. He could hear Tuktu again. Oddly enough, the voice sounded cool, almost amused.

"This thing's tearing down more kelp than they'll harvest."

It was hard to see in the light-streaked water, but clearly the squid had turned direction. Kim fired again and again into the mass. Three-quarters of the creature were arms and tentacles. It would take luck to find head, eyes, and nerve centers.

There was a high-pitched warble, tilting off the edge of sound into a scream.

As Kim watched in horror, he saw a great curved arm come into view. It carried the limp body of Genright. Unconsciously, Kim noted that the young warden's tank and mask seemed to be intact. But Genright's body was rag-flopping, inert. He swam directly into the tangle of deadly flesh.

"Tuktu!" he warbled without thinking. "It's got Genright. I'm making a try for him."

There was no answer.

Then there was, and with it new courage.

Boring through the kelp, swiftly and as directly as aimed missiles and just as relentless, came the dolphins. They homed on the great squid's mantle, their jaws scissoring for the attack. Generations of their cetacean ancestors, particularly their cousins, the whales, had fed upon squid and had borne the scars of arms dappled with toothed suckers for their diet.

There was a single thud of impact. Pudge and Peggy struck simultaneously, driving their weight into the prey. There were tons in collision.

From the edge of his vision, Kim sensed other forms behind the dolphins. Dimly he knew that they must be divers coming from the harvest fleet on the surface with new help. And in the new light they brought with them, he saw Genright's body float loose as the giant arm released it. He swam for it.

The world turned black. The massive struggle vanished. The giant squid spewed forth tons of the inky, ebon fluid concealed within its body for use as a last, desperate escape cover. An acre of the kelp forest became night. Kim reached Genright. He found a grip on a tank strap attached to his shield suit and held on.

Something reached out of the darkness and struck a blow. Kim felt his head snap into his shoulders. And that was the last he felt. But the squid arm that had flicked from the inky cloud to deal that blow curled back upon itself. It slowly settled to the bottom.

There was talk along the bubble network. Back at the base at Baja, Commander Tod Torrance issued instructions. Some of them were reissued by the Harvest Master as the hovercraft fleet began its work in the canopy of the kelp forest. Long booms bristled from the sides of the mother ship, and great bloody sections of giant squid were taken aboard. Some of its flesh would feed the cities. Laboratory workers would analyze other portions of its body, continuing research on the nerve structure begun by other technicians two centuries previous.

The voices were very faraway, but Kim heard them.

"Concussed, wrenched back, sprained shoulder, one broken collar bone, and decompression now complete."

He opened his eyes and looked at the little, brown-faced doctor he had last seen in his bubble with Toby Lee, Dr. Felipe Baguio, he remembered. But something was funny. The doctor had two faces. Tuktu was standing beside him. He had two faces as well. He remembered something else.

"Genright?" he asked through stiff lips.

"Regenerating room," said Tuktu, "for a new arm."

"You're fine," added the doctor. "We got you both up in a hurry, and too fast for the capsule so you had to go back under pressure. That process is now complete. If you can't move, don't worry. I've got you in a stiff gelatin cast."

Kim could almost feel his mind begin to work.

Genright and a new arm, he thought. There were many creatures in the sea with the power to grow new appendages for those lost in combat or by accident. Long study of those creatures over the years had made some of the process available to man. All sea hospitals kept spare parts in their body banks, arms, legs, and other vital organs. Regeneration was a fact, and almost always successful.

"Genright?" he asked again.

"So maybe he'll have a white arm," said Tuktu. "But thanks to you he'll be around for a long time, all of him." He grinned. "You didn't ask how I was," he continued, "and Pudge and Peggy are busy below."

Kim was very sleepy. He slept.

The sun was bright at Baja. It burned the bay waters white, and it turned the sea lemon. In Commander Torrance's office on the spit of land between bay and sea, the light was muted by polaroid windows. But it was ample to see the small smile lines in the commander's face, and to see a companion pleasantry on the face of Assistant Commander Jiggs Jensen.

Kim, a new stripe on his short-sleeved uniform shirt and new creases in his dark green shorts, stood erect before them. He looked at the three people behind them. There were Tuktu, Genright, and, very proudly, Toby Lee with her knees shining beneath a trim skirt that looked as though it were woven from sargassum weed.

"Congratulations, Warden Second Class Rockwell," said Commander Torrance. "As you know, it is customary to serve a certain time in one grade of rank before advancing into another. Your recent conduct in the kelp forest has shortened that time.

"I might add that it was not your response to the Toby Lee emergency or your analysis of poisoned water. Nor was it your obvious concern with your fellow workers in the case of Genright and the squid.

"This is a practical service. And that sort of conduct is expected. But your warning to the surface fleet about to begin the kelp harvest could have saved us considerable equipment. The state of the world being what it is, equipment is hard to come by. . . ."

Assistant Commander Jiggs Jensen laughed.

"So, Warden Second Class Rockwell," continued Commander Torrance, "congratulations. You are relieved of duty in the kelp and hereby assigned to a period of laboratory duty at Baja before reassignment to the beef shark herds in the inshore compounds of Jewel Bay, Baja. Dismissed."

They sprawled on the beach together, Toby Lee, Tuktu, Genright, and Kim, two hours later.

"I don't suppose anybody wants to go for a swim?" asked Tuktu.

"I never learned," said Genright.

"Us neither," shouted Toby and Kim as one.

"Well, Genright and I have one more month in the kelp before we get our stripes," said Tuktu. "Now that you rank us, you'll be awful to live with, Kim. But maybe we can catch an assignment in the shark compounds with you."

"Maybe," said Toby Lee. "Meanwhile he'll be working in the laboratory with me where he belongs. . . ."

"With you?" queried Genright.

"Or some other shark," said Kim firmly.

Book Two
THE SHARK PENS

What was once Baja California before the nuclear war fractured the earth was now a chain of islands. None of them were more than a few miles in width, and most of them were desert supporting experimental groves of dwarf trees, some random miles of transplanted grasses, and blotchy patches of strange bushes bleached by salt and sun.

The sea surged over the islands when the big storms came. And even when it was most docile, the Pacific poured through many inlets into what the old maps in the libraries of the hive cities, burrowed deep in the inland earth, showed as the Gulf of California. There was always the tidal exchange of warm, inshore waters with the cold floods of the open ocean.

It was an exchange which kept inshore water temperatures near 70 degrees on the Fahrenheit scale. It kept salinity readings stable and even currents predictable.

And as Kim Rockwell, Marine Warden Second Class, attached to the Headquarters Marine Base at Baja and the beef shark compounds, well knew, it was a controlled exchange. Each one of the many inlets dividing the chain of islands was a product of skilled hydraulic engineering. Some rationed the tides. Others served as supply funnels

routing food fishes such as the mutated herrings, anchovies, and other migratory stocks from the open sea into
the inner waters.

The ancient gulf had been renamed Jewel Bay. The
name came from the areas of fused earth which rimmed
the shore line of the vast estuary. These ceramic
"beaches," hard fired by fusion blasts, sparkled like jewels
of many colors.

Kim watched the play of sunset light along the eastern
rim of the great bay, a light so clear that the range of
mountains nearly thirty miles away seemed almost within
walking reach. He wore the classroom uniform, short-
sleeved blouse and shorts, deep-depth green in color, and
rope-soled sandals. There was a patient set at the corners
of his mouth. It was a patience shaped by long discipline
and a deserved, if quiet, pride. Not many young men
were Wardens II at seventeen. True, the International
Marine Council took only the best of the candidates selected by the hive city Career Boards for Underwater
Cadet and Warden Training. And he had worked hard
studying the old and new sciences for some ten years.

He was waiting for Toby Lee. He had left her in the
Base Laboratory. She had been scanning sections of the
tough cartilage that made up the backbone of a specimen
beef shark under a tri-dimensional, computer-linked microscope. It was a method of determining age, growth,
and eventual stock weight in the animals. She had wanted
to finish up before joining him at one of the docks which
served the shark compounds.

He squinted at the great bay as he waited.

From its northermost inlet, ranging south for more than two hundred miles to the shallow, land-locked flats of the estuarial farms, which supplied both food and drugs for the cities from many cultivated life forms, Jewel Bay was a monstrous aquarium.

And some seventy miles of its comparatively deep waters to the north were graze and holding pens for the beef sharks.

There were many such establishments throughout the world of oceans in all latitudes, and wherever they could be maintained.

In a world grown arid and chemically polluted long before the crushing ruin of atomic disaster, land areas fertile enough to grow even the meanest of food crops were few. The seas meant survival.

Kim did not dwell on the thought. He watched the light-flecked waters. Beneath them, and en route back to base, were Tuktu Barnes and Genright Selsor, who were now also assigned to the shark pens.

Both were still Wardens III although due for advancement for service time in that grade. Tuktu didn't care about rank. Kim thought it mattered to Genright, however. He sensed a change in Genright since that clash with the giant squid in the kelp forests. If it weren't un-Service-like, he could think that Genright resented the fact that Kim had been credited with saving his life.

But, then again, maybe Genright wasn't too happy in the shark pens. He had been moody and oddly strange since the first days of Baja duty.

The great, fanged selachians could be controlled and

bred. Some species like the porbeagle variants, the herring sharks, in the bay could become domesticated in a wild sort of way. No shark could be made docile or harmless.

The mutated monsters of the open, pelagic range, the great whites which reached lengths of sixty to eighty feet, and the blues, the tigers, the makos, the hammerheads, threshers, lemons, and their assorted cousins could only be taken in open and bloody battle. Usually this demanded sophisticated equipment, and the help of dolphin packs trained to combat.

If Genright were nervous about sharks, let him be, just as long as it didn't interfere with the work. Kim couldn't say that he felt any affection for them. He felt an inside smile at his own nonsense. He certainly wasn't about to go itchy-kitchy-coo or tickly-scratchy-scrutch at any of those ever-moving beasts, which never slept and never rested in the lifelong quest for food.

He remembered one of the first indoctrination lectures given by Base Commander Tod Torrance to the new wardens assigned to the pens.

"The life form we know as sharks goes back to the Devonian period, some two hundred and seventy or three hundred million years ago in earth's history. It is one of the dawn vertebrates. It has adapted and endured, and in many cases with very little physical change. Man as *Homo sapiens*, appearing on earth only a bare million years ago, is an infant compared to the shark.

"Further, man has an inherited fear of sharks."

Commander Tod Torrance was a slatlike man, wiry and

lean, a prototype of physical economy. He had spent more
than thirty years in the International Marine Service.
When he grinned he lighted up a room.

"That comes from long years of being eaten by them,
long years of worshiping them as gods, and only a
comparatively few years of eating them back."

We do more than eat them back, thought Kim. A
portion of their meat goes back to the cities fresh for
ration roasts. Hides go back for leathers and abrasives.
Livers go back for precious oils and vitamins to ease the
burden on the manufacturing laboratories. Fins go back
to be boiled down for gelatin soups. Residues were made
into powder fertilizers to strengthen the nutrients of the
hydroponic farm parks and into protein fish meals for
diet additives. Trace chemicals were isolated for medical
research, and insulin extracts taken from still other organs.

There was a brisk whisper of feet on the dock behind
him.

"Hey, dreamer, here I am at last. Are Tuleta and
Genright back yet?"

He turned and smiled. Toby always looked as fresh
as something just unwrapped, and somehow larger than
a girl who could stand under his outstretched arm.

"Thought you fell asleep. No, Miss Lee. They aren't
back, but maybe the herds were stampeding today."

"I doubt it," she said. "There's enough food in the
bay to keep the darlings in munchies without even moving
for it. The lab charts showed a big school of something,
maybe pilchard, pouring in through most of the north
inlets all day."

"Well, maybe, they're doing range work. Some of those big water filtering sponges that keep the plankters circulating in the South Cove needed relocating a few days ago. And the flat farms had some extra solid wastes from inland to be hauled into the big pens for water enrichment. They'll be along. Look at the other docks."

The docks along the base side of the bay adjacent to Kim and Toby were beginning to show signs of new life as the work crews returned from the open water. Wheeled submarine vehicles of weld glass, awkward with jointed work arms and booms, were crawling up the ceramic rock ramps to the dock runways. They exhaled in snorting whistles as they blew their after hull compression tanks. Those chambers would be reset at the working pressures of the next day for the men using shield suits and tanks. The men now exiting from them, usually in groups of four, began to unload equipment: laser lights, pulsar tubes, drug-guns, sections of glasswire nets, laboratory gear, and assorted tools.

The swimmers, mostly wardens working the near-shore depths, began to pad up the ramps, nearly all of them wearing the silco-membrane, skin-fitting suits which served literally as artificial lungs. Tiny tube follicles from their inner lining penetrated pores to supply the swimmers with oxygen directly from the water and removed the carbon dioxide from the swimmer's bodies at the same time. They were fine for depths down to a few hundred feet, and by the time young sea wardens had served their in-sea apprenticeship they were conditioned to their use.

Seemingly each new generation of Service personnel came born with a little extra musculature about thicker, yet more flexible, rib cages, and a denser layer of muscles over the lower abdomen. Seemingly, the sea changes in the altered oceans applied to the humans who worked in them as well as other life forms.

"Here they come now," said Kim, watching a set of shadows take solid shapes at the dock ramp beneath them.

"And bringing their sheep behind them," giggled Toby Lee.

Kim laughed. Two huge dorsal fins carved tracings in the water surface behind the swimmers. Two more as large but thicker bubbled behind them and suddenly turned into a pair of dolphins which lifted in a burst of foam and grinned at them.

Tuktu and Genright hauled out, kicking off fins and peeling down silco skin to their waists. They saw Kim and Toby, and Tuktu shouted.

"Every day, every minute, my popularity grows. Tomorrow they may follow me into the shower."

He turned and shook a handful of droplets toward the bay.

"Good-by, dear people. Good-by, good-by. Tuktu will see you again. Don't break any teeth until I come."

Kim, half listening to Tuktu clown, noticed a barely perceptible shiver ripple across Genright's shoulders, and a wry grimace cloud his face. Genright did not look happy. He apparently did not think Tuktu was very funny.

"Get cleaned up," yelled Toby. "I've got big news."

"Why didn't you tell me?" asked Kim.

"You had that know-it-all look when I came down, and I didn't get a real buddy smile. You can wait too."

"So there, young hero," chuckled Tuktu, scratching at his chin. "I ought to use some of that sea anenome face wash. Juice from that critter will dissolve a beard right down to your tonsils." He banged Genright on the back. "Good day's work, my skinny one. Let's clean up and eat with these strangers."

Genright said nothing at all.

Toby's big news was apparently everybody's big news in the mess hall. There was more of a buzz than usual hovering over the turtle steaks and garden alva salad.

"We've got a Cryo coming," announced Toby Lee. "He's been in the cities for months taking everything from extrasensory reorientation from the ESPERS to new physical overhaul from the body bank builders. He's making a tour of the Marine bases. What's more, he's one of the original shark experts. His work helped lead to the artificial stock-breeding processes we use in the pens. He's going to lecture here, and work here for . . . well, I don't know. . . ."

"Where did they get him?" asked Tuktu.

"I heard somewhere in the Antarctic. One of the Sea Rovers reported a big iceberg break from an old land mass. An exploration team found a crypt. It was damaged with the exception of one function vault. In it was this Cryo, and fine. His name is Ury Kaane, and they think he's ancient Finnish or Russian."

"How old?" asked Genright, making a face.

"This is only gossip," explained Toby, "but I heard that in biological time he's maybe in his late forties. . . ."

"How about chronological time?" interrupted Kim softly.

Toby hesitated. "I don't know. Before the war, and some say way before that, like late twentieth century or early twenty-first . . ."

Tuktu whistled. There was a grunt from Genright.

Kim shivered, and it wasn't from cold.

"Could be as much as fifteen hundred years?"

They knew about the Cryos. The history machines were explicit, and ever so rarely one or sometimes more appeared to help the cities patch up breaks in the science patterns or lapses in the history data or research gaps in the psychosocial correlations. Some appeared and as rapidly vanished. They were dangers to some phase of life balance in the hive burrows.

The Cryos were the Long Sleepers. Their name came from one of the old sciences called cryogenic interment. It was a deep freeze halt of functional metabolism coupled with complete preservation of all physical organs and cybernetic maintenance of all cell structures. The Sleepers slept away the centuries safe, sound, and intact within the hidden function vaults with only occasional life currents lighting the dormant nerve links within the brain to stir some seldom dream.

The Cryos were stock-piled humanity placed away for the future by governments able to foresee impending disaster for the earth, but unable to halt it. Most of them were geniuses; healers, conservationists, physicists, biol-

ogists, mathematicians, metallurgists, engineers, men to
rebuild future environments, and quite a few women too.
Many of them were young, and many worn with illnesses,
once fatal, which awaited some discovered cure by the
science of future years to come. All of them were vol-
unteers.

Kim remembered one of his old city instructors shaking
his head sadly and saying, "It may be that the world
gained nothing. By the time the science of cryogenic
interment was perfected, it was too late. The poets, for
instance, had disappeared."

The routines of reappearance were always the same.
The Cryos were reorientated, rehabilitated, welcomed
back to society and asked to contribute to it within their
own specialties.

The reborn residents from the past were, for the most
part, cherished.

They were also watched.

Baja Base turned out a welcome for Cryo Ury Kaane.
Assistant Commander Jiggs Jensen, the soft-voiced giant
who served as Commander Torrance's executive officer,
said he hadn't seen so many technicians since the last
big seismic storm and the waves that put the laboratories,
barracks, and outbuildings thirty fathoms below sea level.
That was the storm, he said, that clogged up all the vent
pipes with sea urchins, and when they pumped the flues
dry and blew the living pincushions a half mile out to sea,
the otters thought it was raining free lunch and sent in
a thank-you note. They used an urchin spine and ham-
mered it into the shell of a friendly loggerhead turtle

and pointed him toward shore. His carapace was so hard that they busted up a dozen clam shells banging in the note, and gave the turtle hiccups from vibration in his innards. Assistant Commander Jensen often stretched the truth a bit.

Actually, the technicians did not appear in great numbers. The Service was spread thin in that region, but they were representative. A few miners working the magnesium nodule beds on the continental slope from the deep submergence crawlers got in touch with Base and were picked up by light hovercraft. A few weather people living on the forecast and control buoys came in to meet the Cryo. A handful of wardens got leave from the northern kelp beds. Most of the pelagic herdsmen tending migratory pods of California gray whales couldn't make it. But a delegation of government came down from the Denver hive by freight rocket with some machinery and a load of organic wastes. And wonder of wonders, at least for Kim, a Sea Rover showed up who had intercepted the news off old Peru.

The Sea Rovers were the wide-ranging elite of the Service and the last step up the chain of command before Shore Duty Stations. They were the explorer-intelligence branch, proficient in many of the ocean sciences, and many of their missions were assigned directly by the Council of the Joint Cities.

Someday, someday, thought Kim, I'll be one.

Oddly enough, Toby Lee did not share his ambition or his enthusiasm. When he spoke to her about that goal she shrugged it off or changed the conversation, and some-

times she banged her fists together in a flash of anger.
He didn't know why. After all, there had been and were
female Sea Rovers as well as men.

But, so what, he thought. Right now the entire base
seemed curiously festive.

Cryo Ury Kaane was going to be around for a while.
He would lecture and conduct some laboratory classes.
He would conduct them first, however, for the visiting
technicians. Routines of young wardens assigned to Baja
Base would go on as usual.

"Down with us young," said Tuktu.

"Which is where the work is," added Toby Lee.

"Where the company smiles too much," said Genright
surprisingly.

"And where, according to the schedule signed by Mr.
Jensen in his own handwriting, tomorrow the four of us
will repair and reset some baffle nets," groaned Kim.

"Oh, fun, fun, funny fun, and I thank you, Mr. Jensen,"
muttered Tuktu. "I do need the exercise."

"And if he should hear you," giggled Toby Lee, "you'd
be building lots and lots of new muscles."

Kim thought about that the next day. He could use a
few new muscles.

They had loaded one of the four-man, weld-glass subs
at daybreak with net repair equipment and eased off for
the run down the bay to the sector marked on the work
schedule. They wore shield suits, and would don the
small tanks for water work. The shield suits were more

awkward to work in than the silco skins, but they offered more protection against possible shark bumping.

There are many differences between the sharks, whose skeletons are made of cartilage, and the fishes that have bony skeletons like man's. One of them is that the placoid scales which cover the armorlike skin of the shark are really denticles, or actual teeth. They give the rough hide of most sharks a scratchy surface that can tear and cut a swimmer's flesh even through a silco skin.

Cuts bleed. And so sensitive are the organs of smell in most sharks that even the smallest scent diffusion of blood in the water can assemble schools of sharks seeking food.

Shield suits were better for working in in and around the herds.

There were always some sharks nosing about the baffle nets. That's why the nets were there in the first place.

They were set in grid patterns of deceptive simplicity. They were of varying length, some only twenty or thirty feet in length, and were set at varying depths, some only a few feet from the bottom, others near the surface. Most of them were placed to intersect currents that sharks might want to follow. And their major purpose was to break up big schools. Great concentrations led to trouble in the herds; fights, for instance, and cannibalism among size groups.

The nets also discouraged the hungrier types from ranging too far south in the great bay to the nursery grounds where the females were grouped to have their pups.

It took more than nets to discourage some of them today.

All through the morning, as the two teams strung new anchor lines or substituted new webbing and checked top-net buoys, they had company. Pairs, trios, quartets, and groups of cruisers, some thirty feet long, poked up to supervise the work.

"Do you suppose they're more curious on some days than on others?" asked Toby Lee during a work break in the compression chamber of the four-man vehicle now sitting on the bottom under a hundred feet of water.

"They don't trust us to do it right," said Tuktu.

"They sure aren't helping," added Kim. "And if we want to finish this job, we're going to have to shoosh 'em back from the work area. Two of us can do that while two of us work nets, then we'll change about until the job's done. What do you think?"

"Pulsars," said Toby Lee, "but nice and gentle. This section of bay runs to big ones today, and I wouldn't want anybody out there to get unhappy."

"We'll take herd duty first," said Kim.

"While I sweat and strain and Genright hands me the exact tools I don't need," grinned Tuktu. "Let's get at it, and make sure our communicators communicate. I like to know where everybody is."

"I'd like to be someplace else," muttered Genright.

Kim glanced at him sharply.

Tuktu checked himself and popped out the hatch.

The water was clear and tinged with a silvery green from the high-riding sunlight on the bay above them.

Visibility was excellent; one could count the tiny bubbles of their passage, close-set bubbles because the water was gluey and heavy, and probably high in salt content.

Kim and Toby swam up current from the net Genright and Tuktu were realigning.

Kim checked the communicator in his face mask. He raised both Tuktu and Genright. He reset for Baja Base and checked in with a report.

"Two working, two chasing," he said. "Very nosy down here, and very big noses."

"Read you, Rockwell, out."

Kim changed back to their own warble frequency.

He and Toby carried small pulsar tubes, hand-handy, and about two feet in length. They were variable pitch resonators and could be set to emit sound pulses at any interval and in any selected vibration pattern.

"Very low?" asked Toby, twisting away from a gliding fusiform body that moved like a passing shadow some eighteen feet long.

"Very low," agreed Kim.

The sense of smell is the most acute of all shark senses. It is closely followed by what, in humans, would be the sense of hearing, the ability to detect sounds and vibrations, particularly low-frequency ones. Most fish have that sense and many ocean mammals, especially the dolphins.

In sharks the sensing equipment, which handles most of this sound detection, is known as the lateral line. It runs around the side length of a shark like a horizontal tunnel of nerves. It is a tunnel which sends out sense-collection tubes that end as pores on the outer skin.

The old scientists of the sea suspected that the lateral line was sort of a "radio receiver" which served sharks as a means of long range "touch." They assumed that it also had something to do with the sharks' graceful and eternal swimming balance. They knew that when the nerves which linked the lateral line to the brain were cut, sharks failed to "sense" movements in the water.

Kim and Toby beamed a low-toned, mild buzz from their pulsar tubes as they swam across the path of a few oncoming brutes. It was set at a training frequency, a gently annoying one. The sharks turned, taking their business elsewhere. One of them winked a round blue eye, pulling an eyelid up from the bottom of the eye instead of down from the top, as if to say he really didn't care about nosing into the net at all.

Toby and Kim swam leisurely, easily, and with little bodily movement. Wariness was better than hurry in the great bay. There were always marine types which thought otherwise, however.

"Upstairs," said Toby.

Kim tilted his body. Eighty feet above them a solo sea turtle, looking like a silver coin, some twelve feet in diameter was boiling along in the final stages of some fantastic boat race. All four flippers moved in rhythm like oars. There was wake behind its tail, which was busy as a rudder.

"He's late for a down-bay date," grunted Kim.

"Tag game," said Toby.

Right behind the turtle was a dolphin. It was sizable, some twenty feet long. And it looked as if it had some impish design on the turtle's tail.

"Man, he's goofing off for games instead of minding the store. I wondered when one or more of them would show up."

"All you had to do was warble if you wanted any of them," said Toby.

"Let's keep it peaceful. It isn't roundup time."

Tuktu's voice interrupted them.

"Chat, chat, chat," it said. "There's one more little section of weave to fit, and you two can come do it."

The teams swapped places, Toby and Kim handing over the pulsars in exchange for tools.

"Ought not to be too long now," reported Tuktu.

Kim thought he heard the whisper, although it came thready and more like an impression than a statement.

"Anytime down here is too long."

"You say something, Genright?" he asked.

There was no answer as Tuktu and Genright swam off, and Kim and Toby began to work. Toby was silent.

Kim felt again that vague stirring of uneasiness about Genright. He forced himself to think about it in terms of the Service and his long training. He thought about it in terms of his still comparatively new rank. He put the last tie on a weave of glass netting, went down the anchor line to make certain that the fittings and swivels on the anchor holdfast would be firm and yet flexible enough to take water motion and net banging from even trapped sharks. Once in a while one tangled in the mesh despite the smallness of the weave.

He thought about Genright in terms of Tuktu and their closeness as a team. If anything at all impaired the functioning ability of one partner it could risk the life of the other. The sea does not forgive mistakes. Small errors, and above all the fears which led to them, could end in disaster.

"Anything wrong?" asked Toby in a small voice.

She had the habit of walking right into his mind and sharing it. As she did so again, he wondered if Tuktu shared the same entry to thoughts and feelings with Genright. In-sea buddy teams did. The Service saw to that.

"Yes," he said.

"You'd better fix it."

Kim finished his chore. The water was changing hue. The silvery green of the high sun was deepening into the blue cast of smoke haze, and visibility was dropping with the afternoon descent of the light into the Pacific.

He nodded the communicator to conference call to state the end of the work. As he did so there was a sharp command which almost rattled his mask.

"Turn it, Genright. Turn it!"

Kim heard a sodden thud. He spun in the water to get a look at the up-current side of the net where Tuktu and Genright were discouraging visitors. He heard a rising note drone up the sound scale of the pulsar tube. There was a hissing crunch near the base of the net. A great gray-white shark was turning away, retreating into the water haze.

"It's Tuktu at the base of the net. He's bottomed and he's hurt!" said Toby Lee steadily.

"Come in, Genright," snapped Kim.

He and Toby swam to the sea floor and eased Tuktu into a floating carry. As they did so Genright joined them.

Together they made their way to the work sub.

Tuktu was limp as they pulled him into the compression chamber. He had lost his mask. The compact tank was askew, and Toby removed it. She loosened the fastenings on Tuktu's shield suit. And he shook his head as she did so.

"Wow," he moaned. "Just wow."

"What happened?" demanded Kim firmly.

"Saw it coming and ran into a swipe of that tail," said Tuktu. "Careless, I guess." His voice was low but even and determined.

"I asked what happened," said Kim. "Report, Genright, and now."

"I didn't do the job," he answered. "It was a big one. I was afraid. I got out of its way. Tuktu never saw it at all, I think. It came fast. Not mean. Just fast. When it veered, the tail flicked him."

"Good thing it didn't catch me in the head," said Tuktu, trying to smile.

Kim looked steadily at Genright.

Genright rubbed a weary hand across his face, swiping at its wetness. Some of that wetness was tears.

Kim was suddenly very tired. He looked at Toby. He snapped the communicator to Baja Base. "Job done," he said, fighting a thickness in his throat. "We're coming in.

You might have a doc at the ramp. Tuktu got banged. He might have sore ribs." A tail blow could also kill. . . .

They were a quiet group on the way home, and conversation was brief at the ramp where a medical pickup waited to check out Tuktu who walked stiff-gaited to meet it. They had shed the shield suits for shorts and shirts.

"If you can walk, you can run," said one of the young medical attendants. "At least, you aren't all mincemeaty and horrid."

Tuktu stared at Kim.

"Not me," he said. "The report goes with the rank."

Kim nodded. There was a small twist at the corner of his mouth. Toby noticed it and lifted her hand toward him. Tuktu saw the movement, and understood it.

Genright walked steadily off the dock and never offered a hand with the unloading.

If you can't stop thinking about how to say it, then just think about getting it said because it *has* to be said. Kim was miserable. It was an hour before he made the request to see Commander Torrance, and an aide told him to come right up to the headquarter office. He had avoided the evening meal, and Toby had gone for a walk down the beach so he would not have to avoid her.

There was a handsome blur of smoke-orange light at the far rim of the sea, and it made the commander's desk appear to float as it filled the window behind it. Assistant Commander Jiggs Jensen leaned against a corner of the desk, silhouetted and huge. An onrush of afterglow from the sunset made office lights unnecessary.

"You're late, Rockwell," said Torrance from the dusk in his face.

"Late, sir?" queried Kim.

"I figured it would take you less time. Mr. Jensen disagreed. He ventured that you might not come at all. Mr. Jensen was wrong, which should cause him some embarrassment."

"Well, sir," said Kim.

"As you know, I check all accidents in the pens and all herd mishaps. I happen to think that Tuktu Barnes is a warden of promise. I went to see him. He has three cracked ribs which do not interfere with his appetite. You have nothing wrong with you, but you did not eat dinner."

"Yes, sir," said Kim.

"Tuktu said you would be along. He said that before he told me the whole story of Genright's performance and its cause."

"He did, sir?" Kim felt a flash of heat at the tips of his ears and a blaze of blush at his cheekbones. He was glad the office was not too brightly lighted. The thought occurred to him that his commanding officers were considerate men and that the dimness was deliberate. His face felt hotter.

"Tuktu has been Genright's in-sea buddy for a long time. He is also a perceptive person. And, incidentally, he gives you credit for the same sort of perception. He has known since the first day that he and Genright came to Baja that Genright was afraid of sharks. He has also

known how well and hard Genright has fought himself
to beat that fear. And he is convinced that Genright will
beat it. Have you anything to add?"

"Only that I'm glad Tuktu told you, sir. I might not
have gotten my report exactly right."

"Tuktu didn't think so. He said that you would have
done it justice. Would you care to make any recommendation?"

"I don't know enough, sir," said Kim, "but . . ."

"But what?"

"I think that Genright's fight isn't really all his own.
It's Tuktu's as well, and mine, and it belongs to a lot
of us. But, at the same time, it adds a risk down there
we could do without. But maybe as long as we know
about that risk we could help Genright win his battle."

"Make your recommendation, Rockwell."

"Return him to duty with confidence, sir."

"That's your idea, eh?"

Kim felt reckless. "Not all of it," he said. "Most of it
seems to be Tuktu's."

"We'll consider it, and thank you, Rockwell." Commander Torrance paused. He rattled a rumble around in
his throat, sort of a decision-making noise. He stared at
Assistant Commander Jensen who turned to face him.

"I'll tell him," said Jensen softly. "Rockwell, you may
or may not know it, but Mr. Torrance and I worked as
an in-sea team for many years. We went Rover that way
as well. My Service record so far is sound if not distinguished. I was once moved and reassigned from shark
holdings on another coast because I was petrified at work-

ing with those animals. I still am, and outside of some drastic surgery between my ears, I don't think I'll ever be cured. And if you ever mention one word of this to anyone, you will wind up picking lichens in the polar north for the rest of your career."

"Thank you, sir," said Kim.

"Let's get some lights on in here," said Mr. Torrance. "Good night, son."

Mr. Jensen rose. He flicked on a switch. But as Kim turned to leave there was a knock on the office door.

"Come in," said the commander brightly. "Ah, yes," he added. "Wait a moment, Rockwell."

The man who walked through the doorway was small, stockily compact, and trim in a Service blouse with no insignia. He moved almost daintily. His close-cropped hair was night black. Kim had the impression that his features were regular, if flushed with new sunburn. His eyes as he glanced into the room were bright with interest. They held violet tints.

But as Kim caught and held their direct look they darkened. Kim fought a flinching sensation. He seemed to be gazing through two holes in some remote space, and that space dark, lost, and terribly lonesome.

Those eyes looked across a void and knew emptiness, but only for a shred of a second, and then they sparkled at him.

"Warden Rockwell, this is Mr. Ury Kaane, now assigned to this base for special duty. As the work rotations permit, you and the younger wardens will attend his class and lectures starting, I believe, tomorrow," said the commander.

"How do you do, sir," said Kim.

The man's handclasp was light but firm, and his voice offered a cheerful secret. "Yes," it said, "the Cryo."

"Good night, Rockwell." He was dismissed.

There were lights in the base buildings, but he found Toby Lee sitting in the dark on the steps of the dormitory barracks she shared with a group of female technicians. There was a nearly invisible shape hunched beside her.

"Hi, you," she cried.

"Who's with you?"

"Genright," she answered.

"Well, old Genright can go swipe me something to eat, can old Genright. I missed my dinner on account of old Genright, and old Genright is definitely not all that special to me."

He could hear the relief in Genright's exhaled breath, and Toby Lee's giggle made flute music in the night.

There were not too many in the audience the next morning when Kim and Toby Lee entered the laboratory lecture room. The Baja Base was also a rest and recreation center, and the transients unless specifically assigned were not about to sit indoors. Many of them had already heard Ury Kaane. But there were a group of plankter specialists in from a trawl, a handful of benthic analysts up from the wild life on the bay bottom, a scattering of communications experts torn from their sonar-radar-TV-pulse, beam-heat sensing and electronic networks. There were also Genright and Tuktu, wearing a vest splint of algae gell to ease his ribs.

Kim noticed with some surprise that Commander Torrance and his executive officer Jensen were there, and with them a man wearing dark government garb better suited to the cities than the open marine atmosphere.

"Who's he?" Kim asked softly.

"I have heard that sometimes Cryos are escorted by people who help them to adapt to our ways, and to protect them," answered Toby. "I don't really know, and it could be only a rumor."

Ury Kaane seemed perfectly at home as Commander Torrance introduced him. He was relaxed, poised, and he gave the impression of a man pleased to share professional opinions among professionals. His face showed age lines that Kim had not noticed in Torrance's office, but he stood like an athlete. The violet eyes were bluer today, regarding, if somewhat quizzical.

His voice was wryly gay as he began to talk.

"I am pleased to be in your world with you. My knowledge of it is imperfect. It appears to be better than the one I stepped away from for a nap. It has the advantage of existence. I have been asked, as a natural scientist of the past, to make some comparisons between that past and what I have seen so far of our mutual present.

"The biggest difference I have observed is that this world cherishes its natural environment. It considers human actions in the light of possible consequences upon that environment because it knows that it is essential to human life. My world did not. It perished.

"I can tell you that it would have died without the last war."

"I don't know whether I like my history this way," whispered Toby Lee.

Kim was silent.

Ury Kaane spoke simply. He described how prewar industrial man had polluted the air he breathed by robbing it of oxygen and filling it with carbon dioxide from millions of fuel-burning devices. He described the methodic destruction of millions of acres of growing green plants which could have converted that carbon dioxide into priceless oxygen through photosynthesis. He spoke of the chemical, the organic, and heat pollution of earth's lakes, rivers, and seas which destroyed the micro-organisms which formed the base of the human food chain. He recalled the waste products of the early atomic energy adventures which released biologically fatal isotopes into both soil and atmosphere.

The lab lecture room was hushed to everything but the metronome of Ury Kaane's voice.

He talked of pesticides and herbicides and of precious arable land made salt and useless by desperate irrigation projects that sought to stave off starvation for a world overburdened by too many people.

"The men of my time knew the dangers of environmental destruction," he said. "Children were taught about them in our schools. But man forgot that man was only a part of earth's total life even though its dominant form.

My people risked, and knowingly risked, the survival of man as a species for short-term material comforts and called the process civilization. They lost. Total nuclear war was only an anti-climax."

There was no passion in Ury Kaane's voice, but Kim sensed a thread of pain. There was pride there too.

The Cryo told of the men who, foreseeing the need for human reseeding, had shaped the prototype hive cities. The men who had stocked them and stored them with all of the science and knowledge possible to assemble for those who might come after them.

"This world has endured on much of that science and on the new ones you have created to meet the conditions of a greatly altered natural environment. I am amazed at how much of the old you have kept, and what you have chosen or have been forced to discard, perhaps because of a lack of stable metals. I have not been here too long, but I am told that the remains of what we once knew as a program designed to reach our neighboring planets and stars endures only as a weather control system still in its forecast stages. I am amazed, although perhaps I should not be, how much of earth has yet to be re-explored and its conditions re-examined before the hives which gave the race haven can emerge once more to the sunlight.

"I have assumed that the greatest need is still food supply, although your social sciences and your psycho-medical advances have kept the demands for it within reach of the potential supply."

The Cryo paused. He smiled.

"The sea which gave us birth more than ever gives us life."

Commander Torrance rose as Ury Kaane finished.

"Dismissed," he said. "And I wish Warden Rockwell to remain a moment."

"I'll wait for you," nodded Toby Lee, and rounded up Genright and Tuktu with a wave of her arm and a point to the door.

Commander Torrance was brief.

"Selsor stays on duty without prejudice. Tuktu is pleased. You are pleased. But I am adding Toby Lee to their in-sea team for temporary duty."

He paused. "I didn't see anything special about you last night, but our visitor did. He has asked that you be detailed to him as an aide, sort of a handy type. . . . Did you see anything special about yourself last night that might have caused that request?"

Those lost eyes that saw darkness, thought Kim.

"No, sir," he said.

"One more thing, I want you to meet someone else."

The man in the dark government city suit was suddenly at the commander's elbow.

"This is Mr. Brent, assigned by the Council of Cities to special duty. He too is an associate of Mr. Ury Kaane."

Mr. Brent looked as if he had once commanded something more than wet suit. He was broad in the shoulders and his eyes were sea-green and probing. His voice was soft yet somehow curt.

"Rockwell," he mused. "We shall see something of each

other. Do well." He hesitated. "Cryo Ury Kaane is a valuable guest."

"That's it," said Commander Torrance. "Today play. Duties tomorrow."

They were waiting for him outside the building. Toby was scratching Tuktu's back with a sharp stone where it itched under the gell splint vest, and Genright was figuring out a better method.

"You can take this baby octopus, see, and centrally locate it in the middle of your back, see. Then stand over by the live tank in one of the labs and let it wave to its mother. . . ."

"Suppose its mother was out to lunch when I itched?"

"Suppose Toby Lee was out to lunch?"

"I'd back into a building and wiggle."

"With an octopus on your back?"

"I would have given it a day off."

"That's nice, then it could go out to lunch with its very own mother."

"How about taking me out to lunch?" interrupted Kim.

"You got eight arms?" asked Tuktu.

"I could borrow."

"Not my clean white one," said Genright.

"Two from Toby Lee then."

"Not without marriage," she snapped, "and cut it out! What's with you and the command performance inside?"

"We're divorced. You join Tuktu and Genright who is a man in all-around fine standing while I become an orderly to the Cryo. Shall we all go somewhere and try to figure it out?"

"Not without marriage," grinned Tuktu.

Toby Lee kicked him in the shins.

"Put a gell splint on that," she cooed.

They borrowed a flat-bed beach haul which was nothing but a solar-powered battery on slats usually used to gather kelp hay or haul a meat turtle from the pens. They lurched up several miles of beach to one of the inlets and flopped beside it to watch the sluice boil with incoming food fishes chased from the open sea.

"You met that Cryo last night and he liked you," said Toby Lee, "and he asked for you and he got you. Why you? Just why you? And the special duty Mr. Brent says that Ury Kaane is a valuable guest. I know he's a great pioneer biologist and a shark expert. The labs around here are full of great specialists. What does Mr. Kaane from way back there know that they don't?"

"They'd discover that in the cities. Maybe they think he knows more than he has remembered as yet, something useful. . . ." Kim's voice trailed off. "Or maybe something else."

"Very complicated," said Genright.

Tuktu was thoughtful. "You must have done something to make him ask for you or sensed something."

"Let's forget the whole thing. I have my orders, and I've told you what yours will be when they reach you all nice and formal. Just one more thing for two male wardens around here, let my bubble buddy take care of you down there. She'll keep you out of mischief. Animals like her."

Toby Lee made a face.

Whatever Ury Kaane knew that he hadn't remembered certainly didn't interfere with his work as the days went by. His lectures on comparative anatomy studies were crisp and right from the laboratory to the classrooms. He reviewed the early work which led to selective breeding and the creation of livestock use among sharks. He was vastly interested in what he called accelerative change in the life of the sea, due, as he thought, to atomic bombardment and the shifting alterations in the relations of adjusting factors.

Kim discovered something about the man every day. He learned that the Cryo was a fine diver who adapted to and delighted in the silco skins, shield suits, and the equipment available for in-sea routines.

He learned something else when Ury Kaane first expressed his wish to work in the bay. He learned it from Commander Torrance and Mr. Brent, who were blunt.

"Rockwell, he is your responsibility down there. Make very certain that his science stays sane, that he takes no chances whether he sees risk or not."

But Ury Kaane went among the sharks as if he owned them, and with deftness and surety. He turned Kim's mind inside out learning actual processes, forcing Kim to learn more in order to teach the Cryo.

The shark pens, quite literally most of the more than seven thousand square miles of Jewel Bay with the exception of the shallow farms at the landlocked south, were simply one big stock-herding operation. The entire north end of the bay held the "beef" males which when they reached maximum size and girth were rounded up and prepared for market. The middle portion of the bay was the harem where once a year the females were herded to and spun through mating enclosures and artificially "seeded" through the ingenious use of false claspers.

This was dangerous work. It was made less hazardous during the mating season by mild diffusions of nerve gas, worked out to laboratory formula and seeped into the bay waters by divers, all of them working with tanks. The sharks' highly developed scent mechanisms provided their own anesthesia, enough to make them reasonably torpid. But not enough to halt their swimming abilities. A shark must live by constant motion and with a constant flow of water taken through its mouth to enrich its slit gill rakers with oxygen.

Once mated, the females were herded back to the harem. From there, in due course, they were moved again to the shallow nursery grounds to bear their litters, dropping young fully equipped to fend for life at birth. And there too the pups were separated according to the sexes for relocation.

The bay herds were a product of long breeding efforts, and so-called "standard stock." But no effort of man had ever made the shark anything less than a marvelously weaponized stomach forever in search of food, and ferocious in the quest.

Man's control over them was never taken for granted. Even with dolphin assistance, even with the pulsars, stun-guns, lasers, and the dilute gases, even with ample supplies of food in the bay, there was danger in the shark pens. There were unpredictable and bloody frenzies in the herds. There were cannibal attacks. There were accidents.

Ury Kaane in one of his many conversations with Kim once said, "The nature of evolution is that no species can stand still. It goes forward evolving into something. It can never go back. But I think that the sharks defy that process or else nature took three hundred and fifty million years to catch up to the survival equipment sharks came with at creation.

"Look at those teeth," he continued, banging on a specimen head in the laboratory. "Here are five rows in the upper and lower jaws. They are on active duty. Behind them lying in grooves deep inside the jaw are row after row of reserve troops. When a tooth is broken, smashed or lost, another moves right up to replace it from an endless escalator. And more teeth are developing at the same time to join the reserves. And all that from the beginning of the beginnings. . . .

"Look at that jaw, each one hinged at the center, and each one jointed again at the corners of the mouth. Man, when that mouth is open it could take a whole horse." He paused and said softly, "I wonder what ever happened to the horses?"

One of the many discoveries Kim made and enjoyed about the Cryo was his way of interrupting his own thoughts with other little secret thoughts, many of them meaningless to Kim.

There was a day when they were walking along a portion of beach blotched with sparse grasses. Ury Kaane flopped on the crystalline sand and placed an ear among them.

He listened long and cocked an eye up at Kim.

"No insects," he said. "No rustles, hums, buzzes, chirps. When they are heard again . . . ah ha. . . ."

There was another time they watched a session of gulls convened about a small tidal pool.

"Sea birds, yes, and that's good," said Ury Kaane. "But somewhere in the world there has to be a place where birds sing."

Kim was spending a lot of time with the Cryo, not only in his classes which he attended as a student with Toby Lee, Genright, and Tuktu, but in the working lab keeping records, in the bay among the sharks as Ury Kaane made his insatiable observations, and often during off hours walking and loafing.

Occasionally, Commander Torrance and Mr. Brent would ask him questions about the Cryo. They were circular questions, thought Kim. They were questions which just sort of went around and around in search of something to seek. Commander Torrance showed no signs of changing Kim's duties. In fact, he seemed pleased with Kim's relationship with Ury Kaane.

"His reports on you make me think you may turn out to be some sort of special credit to the Service someday," he told Kim.

Toby Lee took a different view.

"You're no credit to me," she said. "When are you going to come back to work?"

"Why?" asked Kim. "You having trouble with Tuktu and Genright?"

"Noooooooo," she admitted. "But Genright's still sort of uncertain, and somehow any job takes longer for the three of us to do than two of us used to be able to manage. Frankly, with that thing he has about sharks . . . Well, he's got me looking around too. . . ."

Kim smiled at her. "When you look around, imagine I'm right behind you. Temporary duty is called temporary because . . ."

"It lasts so long," snapped Toby Lee. "I'll have to think up a drastic change."

Toby did not have to bother.

There were odd streaks in the sky over the Pacific the next day at dusk as if a giant had made an immense sandwich of violently colored smoke and rested it on the table formed by the horizon, as Kim and Ury Kaane left the laboratory. The air had a strange tart taste. The sea beneath it, while slick and queerly still, was broken by what looked like pockmarks of miniature boilings.

"Odd, very odd," mused Ury Kaane.

Kim felt a faint, faraway ringing in his ears.

The boilings on the sea became geysers. The ground was suddenly snatched from under them and they were spilled to an earth which rippled, rose, and fell like a wave. There was a sound like the loudest bass note of all time which turned into a booming rumble of drums from somewhere deep in the heart of the ground.

A corner of one of the barracks buildings tilted and fell.

Kim staggered to his feet in time to see the surf lift into a single wall of water and surge over the barrier island to wash white water into the bay.

The rumble faded, leaving his ears twanging, and the ground beneath him steadied. The sky spun back into place.

He ran to the sprawl that was Ury Kaane and lifted him to his feet where he swayed, dazed, but apparently uninjured. Kim held him steady and looked anxiously into his face for signs of harm.

The Cryo's eyes seemed to be staring into eternity with that same wide, lonesome probe into blackness Kim had seen before, a probe which found some unspeakable pain and loss. Ury Kaane's lips moved and tried for words.

"Earthquake," shouted Kim. "Bad tremor. This coast has a history of them."

"Bobby, Bobby," said the Cryo distinctly. "You went to the shelter city in Hawaii with your mother, the volcano city beneath the two mountains before I went away . . . before I went away. . . ."

Kim was a product of Service training and discipline. He knew shock when he saw it. He slapped the Cryo's tortured face.

The black light lifted from Ury Kaane's eyes. He shook his head and recognized Kim.

"I'm all right," he said.

There were people running toward them. One of them was Mr. Brent who led Ury Kaane away. One of them was Toby Lee who grabbed both Kim's hands and held them tightly.

Baja Base was landscaped with litter, but it functioned. It coped with cleanup during the night, estimated quake damage, and patched its physical wounds. It tested its communications and examined its equipment and prepared for a survey of the shark pens in the morning. It slept in the end, but not before Kim asked for an interview with Commander Torrance.

He found the commander with Mr. Brent, and asked about Ury Kaane.

"Why now, Rockwell?" The commander was curt.

Kim glanced at Mr. Brent. He was certain that at last he had the answer to all those circular questions. He squared his shoulders stubbornly.

"I hope he's well, sir," he said steadily. "He thinks that I am his son and that I am with my mother in one of the cities named Hawaii."

Mr. Brent's lips tightened. His voice was soft but cold as a drifting berg.

"That's it," he said. "He had to know it. The psycho examinations showed something hidden. But in the Council of Cities there is no Hawaii . . . recognized or known. . . ."

He made a small motion to Commander Torrance.

"Thank you, Rockwell. You are dismissed," said the commander.

Baja Base rested but briefly. The sun had just lifted above the eastern scarps of the bay to put a pewter sheen on the ripples when all warden personnel went on full alert. The first reports from the crews checking possible quake damage in the shark herds brought news of slaughter, of blood-scarlet waters.

The voice which brought the very first report was never heard again. But the communications network had the word.

A pack of orcas, the killer whales, usually found in colder, northern waters, had raided south and entered the bay through a quake-damaged inlet, apparently pursuing a herd of seals.

Kim, restored to in-sea team status with Toby Lee, tried to remember what he knew about killer whales. They were relentless and fierce meat eaters who preyed upon the giant baleen whales, seals, walruses, fish, sea birds, and, like the sharks, even man. The ancient texts described specimens up to forty feet in length and spoke of their immense speed and strength. The pelagic herdsmen had encountered them in mutant variants up to ninety feet.

Orcas were not misnamed. They were killers with rending, conically pointed teeth, and they killed.

Toby and Kim joined Genright and Tuktu at the dock for hovercraft drop-off into their assigned work zone. They wore shield suits with helmets instead of masks. They carried tanks, one of them only a slim, tubular fitting to the air tank which contained nerve gas under pressure. They were armed with laser tubes to be used as both a light source and weapon. Compact pulsars rested in leg sheaths. Drug-guns were left behind. They would take too long to affect killer whales when fractions of seconds counted.

Hopefully, the two-man jet subs powered by A-energy packs would handle actual combat with the orcas. They fired spreads of penetrating pencil darts designed for low intensity explosion within the bodies of great bulk animals. Of course, widespread gas diffusions could be laid to destroy the killers. Ultrasonic emissions and a variety of paralytic poisons were available. But their use would demolish the herds and much of the benthic life as well.

Kim noticed two wardens in silco skin suits wearing artificial squid mantles, sort of a flexible, armored tube which contracted and expanded under power units to "inhale" water and "eject" it from the rear of the mantle. The diver was thus a one-man, jet-propelled unit and capable of high swimming speeds. The two wardens using mantles were assigned to roving duties where needed.

By the time Kim and Toby and Tuktu and Genright boarded the hover vehicle the base sensing scans had pinpointed the location of the killer whale pack. It was amuck in the north beef herd, and when the four of them made their water entrance south of the carnage, the currents were murky with blood.

Their mission was to divert blood-wild sharks leaving the northern frenzy, where the orcas killed at will and panicked sharks killed each other, from entering the harem grounds in any numbers. They were to slay if necessary. If necessary and possible they were to deter pursuing killer whales, should any escape sub attacks.

"Set your buoyancy for midwater," ordered Kim, "and

use manual controls to alter the mass of your weights for fast depth changes. Spread out and cruise and use lights. Everybody all right?"

"I'm sleepy," said Tuktu.

"I'm happy to have a buddy," warbled Toby Lee.

"What are you, Genright?" asked Kim.

"Chicken," came the reply.

Two halves of two great sharks drifted and bobbed below them, one a head section, the other bearing a limp caudal fin.

"Double chicken," said Genright.

"Take no chances," commanded Kim. "Notch laser up to weapon strength when you see anything at all. And set communications to all bands now. We'll know what's going on up there, and we can still hear each other."

Visibility was good, for the most part, from the high morning light on the bay surface above them, but it was patchy with both large and small clouds of stain.

A twenty-foot shadow lanced from one of them directly above Kim, and he sliced its length with the laser beam which bored a small, boiling hole of heat in the water.

"One," he said through the helmet intercom, "watch for more behind him."

A school of foot-long anchovies passed over them like silver tinsel, blown south with their white underbellies gleaming. An oversized harbor seal, a long way from any port, made diligent speed on the surface.

A babble of command, countercommand, and instruction between the jet subs now attacking the orca pack filled their helmets.

"Call those dolphins home. What are they doing in this mess?"

"Count twelve killers in pack."

"No count shark dead from all causes, but herd milling in frenzy."

"Circling outside, well outside the killing grounds," reported one of the squid-mantle jet divers. "No stragglers. No whale stragglers, that is. Some sharks leaving, headed south."

Minutes later Tuktu turned one of them with a scorching slant of laser and it angled for some distant shore line as if to beach itself. Genright intersected another and beamed it dead with an angle shot across its snout.

"Mighty fancy," cheered Toby Lee, seeing the action.

"Stay alert," snapped Kim. "The big fight ought to be breaking up."

"I hope the subs won," said Tuktu.

Three monsters swimming nose to tail in a fleeing chain passed between Kim and Toby. With intuitive teamwork each refused a shot for fear of hitting each other. The sharks banged over a barrier net and glided away.

A voice shrilled into their helmets. "One orca loose from the pack and headed south fast, mad and wounded. Suggest intercept wardens prepare . . . prepare . . . prepare. . . ."

"To go back to bed," suggested Tuktu.

"Close up, close up," said Kim. "We'll split as we see it, if it comes down this track. Might confuse it."

Although he knew Base was monitoring all exchanges, he set the communicator direct to dispatch and command center. "Rockwell here, south zone direct of herd action. No sight of killer as yet."

"Rockwell!" The voice was unmistakably Commander Torrance's. "Get your patrol out of there. Do it now. Do not, repeat, do not attack that thing. Subs can deal with it later. . . . Confirm."

"Too late, sir," snapped Kim. "It's here and . . . here. . . ."

It came like a streamlined avalanche driving through the clouded water with tragic beauty, its mouth agape and its fluke driving. The dead-black silk of its giant back, broken only by the white oval over its eyes, was torn with a raw red gap behind its huge and proud dorsal. There was another red rent of ruin in its shining white belly.

The killer was a wreck of flesh, fully sixty feet long, yet still full of titanic strength and dedicated fury.

It saw them, and without changing its headlong course charged straight for the grouped swimmers, its lidless eyes fixed and baleful.

"Break," cried Kim.

It was too late to spread.

Genright did not attempt to move laterally. He drove forward head on to meet the charging animal, his laser beamed directly into its open maw. As the killer angled upward to escape the pain, Genright dived beneath it, his laser tube held upright, cutting a direct route along the great beast's belly, slicing, burning, and opening a crimson cavern from head to tail fluke.

Before the creature could spin to meet its tormentor,

three other laser tubes focused upon it and held their beams steady upon its mass.

Kim saw his light drive an ever widening hole into the killer at the joint where flipper met body.

The killer's head seemed to tilt away from its body as he watched. The great spiked teeth banged shut, and as life left the orca it seemed to collapse in upon itself, then separate into a spill of spare parts which littered the sea around it. The water turned dark red, and as the monstrous carcass rolled it wrapped streamers of crimson about itself and, veiled within them, sank to the bottom.

"Let's get out of this blood," yelled Toby Lee. "I don't want more visitors attracted this way."

"How about my old skinny buddy, Genright?" cried Tuktu. "How about that old fierce fella? Right into the hole like an eel on a reef! Did you know that killer whales are tougher than sharks, old skinny buddy?"

"Do I have to compare?" asked Genright, and there was a lofty cadence in his voice.

"Probably all day," said Kim, "or at least until all the stock is doped into peaceful cruising."

"Wrong, Rockwell," cut in the drawling precommand voice of Assistant Commander Jiggs Jensen back at Base. "I gather from your youthful chatter that Genright Selsor conquered all. But I digress. You are ordered to surface for pickup and return."

"I knew they'd remember my cracked ribs," chuckled Tuktu. "Will you scratch my back, Toby?"

"Genright will. He can do anything," said Kim, "and to anything anytime."

"Well, it's a mighty nice day for it," answered Genright.

"You won't have any more real bad ones," said Tuktu soberly.

"Not the kind I had before anyhow, old square-shaped buddy," agreed Genright.

Mr. Brent and Cryo Ury Kaane happened by the dock as they landed and managed a greeting. Then they stood solemnly and surveyed the young wardens as though they were measuring them for new silco suits. They appeared to be in silent conference.

Assistant Jiggs Jensen came by to watch them remove gear. He walked down to the ramp edge and tapped Genright on the shoulder.

"Congratulations," he said.

"Thanks," nodded Genright sincerely.

Kim resumed his duties with the Cryo the next day, and for some reason Tuktu, Genright, and Toby Lee were assigned additional laboratory work which kept them under Ury Kaane's instructive eye and out of shark-pen duty.

"Always a switch in this Service," commented Tuktu.

"I don't mind," said Toby Lee, poking a finger into an ear in a distinctly undainty gesture.

Kim wondered and said nothing at all.

A week later he was summoned to Commander Torrance's sea-view office, and again the all-places-all-the-time Mr. Brent was there. He took over the meeting as if he stood on a ship's bridge.

"You will remember your report of events on the night of the quake. Cryo Ury Kaane has since, and with some assistance, recalled more about what he calls Hawaii shelter. An archipelago by that name shows on the ancient charts of the Pacific as a considerable chain of Volcanic islands."

He paused thoughtfully.

"I need not elaborate, but in the past two years we have had Rover reports of what might be called odd happenings in that area of the seas. Not enough to be certain, but enough to indicate that there might be directed activities throughout that section of the range which we are not directing.

"We intend to conduct an elaborate search of the area. Mr. Kaane will accompany that search, enthusiastically, I might add. He has requested that you be assigned to accompany him. Comment, Mr. Torrance?"

The commander picked up evenly.

"You will hold your Warden II rank, Kim," he said, "but you will be designated as being on Rover duty. As you know, this is both an unusual move for the Service and a great compliment to you. It is also a major opportunity for you. . . ."

There was war within Kim. He felt a surge of exhilaration and great excitement. He felt a sickening sense of loss and a sadness. The opposing forces fought for expression upon his face and were clearly seen.

Commander Torrance smiled, and the stiff Mr. Brent produced an antique, patently little-used chuckle.

"When the Service makes an unusual move it moves quite unusually," instructed the commander. "At Mr. Brent's request and by his order as the representative of the Council of Cities, we are also detailing Barnes, Selsor, and Lee to the same assignment."

Kim spun on his heel, remembered, spun back and snapped to attention and saluted. "Request permission to tell them, sir."

"Dismissed," said Torrance gravely.

"When the Service makes an unusual move it moves quite unusually," bayed Kim at the quarter moon sneaking across the sky trying not to awaken the sea in its passing.

"Line up, gentlemen, for one sisterly kiss apiece," sang Toby Lee.

"I wonder what's out there," wondered Genright.

"Wild, nasty, uneducated pelagic sharks," said Tuktu. The same stern thought silenced them simultaneously. The sea range was out there.

Book Three
THE ROVERS

The Sea Warden Service administered by the International Marine Council had its rituals of formality. The Marine Base at Baja in what was once Lower California before the nuclear war and succeeding centuries altered the earth knew all about them.

"Did we get any? No, we did not," grunted Kim Rockwell, Warden Second Class now attached to temporary Rover duty. "What did we get? I'll tell you what we got. Toby Lee kissed by Commander Tod Torrance and Executive Officer Jiggs Jensen. Warden Third Tuktu Barnes and his in-sea buddy Genright Selsor of the same rank got handshakes and a hug around the shoulders. I got handshakes and a couple of jabs in the stomach. Some big formal transfer of duty routine, I'd say."

"Somebody wished us luck, didn't they?" asked Toby Lee.

"That was me," said Tuktu.

"What kind?" asked Genright suspiciously.

"I did the wishing. You have no choice."

"I also got pinched," added Toby Lee thoughtfully. "Twice."

"Only once was me," grinned Genright.

Kim laughed, then sobered thoughtfully.

"I think we're a little nervous," he said, "and maybe we ought to be."

They were skimming north in a high-speed, coast patrol combo-flight hovercraft whose hull, sprouting retractable lift-wing surfaces, whispered through the still air as it consumed great bites of distance.

The variable glare, topside of the trim, weld-glass craft, sprayed an even light upon them as they sat relaxed. It made their deep-green coverall uniforms seem darker, rippled highlights on their polished shark-leather half boots.

"Are you asleep?" asked Genright.

"Why?" queried Kim.

"Your eyes were open," said Tuktu.

"I was thinking," Kim muttered.

"I think with my eyes closed," Tuktu said loftily, "that way I can catch a nap."

"Okay, let me drop off for a short think," snapped Kim.

Anything could happen on an in-sea assignment, and none of them had worked the wide water infinities of the pelagic range. That range belonged to Rovers or Rover Herdsmen—not Wardens, and not usually to those without long seasoning and more than a few years in the Service.

"We can thank the Cryo," said Toby Lee.

Kim started. It was uncanny how often her thoughts paced his own, marching gently, if unbidden, into his mind. But it never failed to surprise him. He knew that Genright and Tuktu shared a similar closeness of perception about each other. And he was beginning to suspect a deep awareness among all four of them which did not need expression, deepened, perhaps, by shared danger in both the kelp forests and the shark pens.

"For this nice patrol buggy ride," mused Tuktu.

"For Rover assignment years ahead of making it the hard way," grunted Genright.

"I wonder what it's like being a Cryo," muttered Toby Lee.

Kim remembered the first time he had met Cryo Ury Kaane in Commander Torrance's office, and that brief, unguarded revelation in the man's eyes which cried of pain, loneliness, and some secret knowledge of the long, black reaches of endless time.

"It isn't easy," he said.

"I think you're right," said Tuktu. "For instance, I can't remember whether or not I put socks on this morning. How about if I had memories maybe fifteen hundred years long to worry me?"

"It was one of those memories that he didn't really know he had that got us this assignment," reminded Toby Lee.

Kim nodded uneasily. In his mind was a vivid picture of the night at Baja when the earthquake rocked the Base shocking the Cryo into a dazed recall of a hidden hive city called Hawaii. He saw again Ury Kaane, memory tortured by a son he thought was Kim and a long-gone wife left somewhere beneath two, vaguely remembered mountains. And then Mr. Brent had taken over.

Mr. Brent had been a mystery man on the Baja Base.

All Kim and Toby and Genright and Tuktu knew about him was that he was a stern and formal representative of the all-powerful Council of Cities on special duty. They now knew that Mr. Brent's special duty was the Cryo. The psychos of the cities knew that Ury Kaane's great mind had not yielded all it held from the years before the Long Sleep. Mr. Brent's job was to watch, wait, and protect the Cryo until it did.

Mr. Brent's job was many jobs, and all of them important, thought Kim. He was command type, and big command too, big enough to have four unimportant wardens designated to highly special duty on his own request and the Cryo's wish for their company.

"I'm hungry," said Tuktu.

A voice from the control center beyond the bulkhead, which divided center from the passenger compartment, said, "I heard that."

"Snoop us some food then," flipped Genright, "you snooper."

"The food lockers under your seats are heating now," said the voice. "Chow ready in five minutes."

"Something tasty for us important people, no doubt," ventured Tuktu.

"Ha," said the voice.

"Which means?" asked Toby Lee, wrinkling her nose.

"Standard awful," replied the voice.

It was abalone steak and delicious. They ate while the patrol craft fled north, and the sea was a thousand seas below them as each cloud shadow, each quarreling breeze, and each current set printed varying colors and patterns on the waters.

They were following the coast, and the long-changed seas, fed by polar and antarctic melt, washed and broke against the scarps of low mountains. There was nothing human on the landscape, but along the scattered miles ridges of green, growing vegetation fought for life against the still tainted soil. Seals played on the rock islands that once marked hills called San Francisco on the old maps, and still they moved northward.

It was nearly dusk when they splashed to a landing at Olympia Base. Kim had an impression of many vast docks, buildings, winking lights, and the murmur of much activity as they eased into a dockside berth among a line of similar craft.

Their pilot slid back a section of bulkhead and stuck a grin-crinkled head at them.

"Out cargo," he said. "Take your hand gear with you. I would be dead wrong to assume that somebody will meet you, especially if somebody's supposed to stow you away. But who knows? Maybe you're planned to be permanent dock standers, ornaments loitering around until the end of time."

"Think of us that way when you have a lonesome moment," laughed Tuktu.

"I will think about the cute one among you," leered the pilot.

"I will think of you too," said Genright solemnly.

"Okay, clown it out of here," said Kim briskly.

Toby Lee waved a pert good-by.

They were met. Ury Kaane met them, small, compact, and trim in a Service uniform without insignia. He ran a hand through his close-cropped, black hair, and the smile in his violet eyes lighted his face. He looked bouncy for a man apparently in his middle forties, somehow eager, and not at all like a famous marine biologist past and present. His smile embraced them as a unit, and if it were a trifle warmer for Kim, he didn't attempt to hide the fact.

"Well, staff members," he said, "welcome to Olympia and great work in progress."

There was a uniformed Service commander with him, his rank showing on his shoulders and a pair of dolphins bright woven into his blouse over his left breast.

Dolphins, the ancient, generation-haunted, tradition-proud sign of the submarine service.

"This is Commander Cassius," said the Cryo.

In a single formal motion, Kim, Toby Lee, Tuktu, and Genright snapped to a rigid second of salute.

It was formally returned.

"Easy, youngsters," drawled the commander.

He was a tall man with a craggy face and a wide, generous mouth. His nose was pug and his eyebrows flared like two black wings above alert, blue eyes. A shock of snow-white hair escaped from the rim of a pushed-back uniform cap.

"Easy," he repeated. "I'm only taking the air with Ury. He wanted to meet you, and I figured I might as well take a look at some new crew at the same time."

"New crew, sir?" asked Kim.

"We are assigned to the Service Laboratory Submarine *Polaris*," said the Cryo quietly. "You know the mission is Hawaii Search, and those detailed to it are now quartered aboard. Commander Cassius is the skipper of *Polaris*. Mr. Brent is the overall command coordinator for the expedition. I am his assistant. As you know, Mr. Brent has assigned you four as my aides at my request back at Baja. I assume you'll also have other duties and disciplines according to routine Service regulations."

"Before everything gets explained to the point of utter confusion," said the commander gently, "just remember that this mission is not a routine one in any sense. Your presence is hardly routine as far as the Service goes, as all of you know." He paused and smiled. "I suggest, however, that you run whenever you are told to run by almost anybody aboard with the possible exception of some of the civilian science people who probably won't notice you anyhow. All clear?"

"No, sir," said Kim, "but we'll do our best to be useful."

"The record indicates as much," nodded the commander. He looked at Toby Lee thoughtfully. "There are female technicians all over the place, Warden Lee. You will be quartered with some of them."

"Shall we go," suggested Ury Kaane.

The commander led the way off the dock to a waiting yard vehicle which took them nearly a mile through Olympia Base roadways to the berth of the *Polaris*.

She was long, sleekly humped and tuna-shaped, with a dull gray iridescence rippling along her hull. Nothing marred her topside, but an entrance hatch poked an invitation to the dock from the upper portion of her shoulder curve.

"Wow!" breathed Kim.

The commander smiled appreciatively.

"Gets you, eh? I'm glad. She's the latest type for her job. Five hundred feet. Radial filament, balanced stress, weld-glass pressure hull tested to more than 250,000 pounds per square inch. Nuclear powered all the way with in-hull sea engines, induction coils driving her on water jets, and the newest anti-gravity keel running her full length."

He chuckled at Toby Lee's puzzled face.

"Not really anti-gravity. We're not that far advanced. The keel's one of the new, stabilized metals with the amazing property of changing molecular densities when we apply energy. Its general mass stays the same, but its weight can be changed in any section along its length at a given time, or its total weight can be altered enough to bottom us at any depth or change total boat weight so we can surface or hold or hover. No more of those old-time ballast tanks, and no more depending upon propulsion to keep us at depth."

"How about speed, sir?" asked Kim.

"Very ample," grinned Commander Cassius, "or none. We call the shots. Further, it has a fully controlled environment below with all the acoustical and vision devices, constant video recording, and biological snoopers our science divisions can handle."

"You're all divers so there are in-hull pressure bubbles for any depth exits and entrances. Oh, she's a beauty."

"How's the food?" asked Tuktu.

Kim jabbed him in the ribs.

"Let's get aboard," said the Cryo firmly. "You'll be assigned quarters and food times. We leave tonight, and Mr. Brent has scheduled an all-boat briefing session for right after general mess."

Commander Cassius led the way.

Kim, Tuktu, and Genright found themselves located in a compartment about midship in a section designated for biologists with the Cryo Ury Kaane bunked alone beyond the adjoining bulkhead. Toby Lee joined two girl technicians, nutrient specialists about her own age, in a compartment across the passageway from them.

"More space than I thought," said Kim, throwing his gear in a locker.

"Pure luxury," grinned Tuktu.

"Compared to what?" asked Genright.

"A sea-floor bubble, that's what," said Tuktu.

They changed into static-free coveralls at Ury Kaane's orders. The Cryo led them to mess in a forward compartment which seated about twenty people, most of them civilian scientists, whom from that time onward they seldom saw except at meals.

They were still at the seat benches when the end wall of the compartment flickered into light and the face and figure of Commander Brent appeared. He too was clad in sea-green coveralls. He spoke crisply and without ceremony.

"As all of you know, this mission is called Hawaii Search, a hunt for a hive city long lost to us in an area which, frankly, we knew little about until recently. It may be something more.

"For more than a year now the Council of Cities has had reports of unusual events from the area we intend to explore. Rover Herdsmen have recorded odd temperature changes and sonic phenomena which have diverted whale migrations from normal patterns. Two manned weather and biological buoys vanished from approximately the same region. Three cybernetic barges seeding currents with new plankter species never homed back to the mother laboratory from that area. Worse, we have had the unpleasant duty of listing an unusual number of veteran Rovers as missing while last reported in what we believe was this part of the Pacific.

"In short, we have long suspected that there might be directed activities in a vast sector of the sea which we were not supervising.

"It may not be likely, but it is possible that such direction comes from a hive city long lost to our knowledge until Cryo Ury Kaane recalled it into being.

"It is our clear duty to investigate. At this moment Commander Cassius is giving sailing orders. That is all."

"It's plenty," muttered Kim. He lifted his glance and caught a shadow of some haunting pain in the Cryo's eyes as the man shifted uneasily in the seat opposite him. Those violet eyes were amazing, he thought. They must be the only such eyes in the world.

For the next day or so the *Polaris* cruised unhurriedly as an oceanic loafer, mostly at depths ranging from fifty to two hundred feet. Occasionally it surfaced to sprout sensory gear for a variety of readings. Now and then it laid a clutch of current and drift data bottles, each of which would emit recordable signals until timers ordered them to self-destruct.

The civilian members of the expedition kept to themselves in their own work divisions. The Service crew, relatively few in number, appeared occasionally and then vanished into hatches and companionways. Commanders Brent and Cassius were like genial ghosts, their presences felt, but invisible.

Kim, Tuktu, Genright, and Toby Lee spent most of their waking hours with Ury Kaane and an assortment of old maps and reference spools.

"We're back in school," said Genright, and in a sense they were. The Cryo was an enthusiastic teacher.

"Nobody knows for certain what today's Pacific floor looks like," said Ury Kaane. "The old charts give us an idea of what they knew about it when Hawaii city was dug shortly before my interment.

He pointed out that the Pacific contained earth's greatest heights and depths, most of them covered with a heaving mantle of sea. The Mariana Trench, as mapped on the old charts, was a deep of 35,800 feet. The big island of Hawaii itself was really a monstrous peak rising 32,024 feet from the ocean floor.

"And between two volcanic peaks on that great single peak," he added, "they dug and shaped the lost burrow city."

The Cryo explained that the Pacific floor held hundreds

of mountain ranges, thousands of seamounts and major faults which were really fractures in the earth itself. Using the old charts, he pointed out many of the extinct, flat-topped volcanoes called guyots.

"Some may even have become reactivated," he said. "Among other oddities in the exploration area there have also been unexplained fish kills. Some of the Rovers have reported schools of dead fish covering miles of sea surface."

When Kim, Tuktu, Genright, and Toby were not with Ury Kaane, they asked for and were given permission to explore the submarine.

Diver crewmen showed them different-sized pressure bubbles in various areas of the boat's inner skin.

"All gear for any kind of dive is stowed within them," explained a young ensign. "As you know, when the in-boat pressure is adjusted to that of the outside sea, and you too are ready, an outer hatch opens right through all hull skins. It stays open until you come back just in case you want to come back in a hurry and don't have time to knock at the door. . . ."

"I holler all the time," interrupted Tuktu.

"To get in," finished the ensign with a grin.

Commander Cassius himself took them about the boat one day.

He showed them the con area with its banks of instruments along the upper swell of the boat's nose.

"Everything computer controlled and automated from navigation to cooking," he said. "You may have noticed in historic pictures that submarines once carried big upper-deck structures called 'sails.' We don't need that dorsal fin effect. We don't even need all the room they once needed within the boat. The anti-gravity keel effect takes care of all stabilization including lateral roll. Equipment miniaturization takes care of inner space problems."

Commander Cassius showed them the boat's magazine.

"All standard sea arms," he said. "Lasers, nerve gases, pulsar tubes, animal anesthetics, small explosives for certain types of bottom work." He paused. "And there are two forms from the archives and the history of earth's destruction." He pointed to two torpedoes some twenty-five feet in length. "They can swim or they can fly. They carry nuclear warheads with enough bang to move mountains."

"Are they ever used, sir?" asked Kim.

"Well, to my knowledge similar ones have been used twice in my lifetime, and both for the same objective. They boomed away at the polar ice cap to dislodge bergs which could be towed southward as water supply for one of the cities during a breakdown in the burrow water system.

"They are," continued the commander, his eyebrows flaring wing-shaped above his pug nose, "an outlawed weapon, and forever so, I hope."

"Do all boats carry them, sir?" asked Toby Lee.

"No," said Commander Cassius.

"Why us then?" queried Kim.

"The answer to that, my boy, lies in the fertile mind of Coordinator Commander Brent and the equally fertile minds of the Council of Cities. Don't you kids have some place to go?"

"Not recently," mused Genright.

"We do now," said Kim.

A speaker from a wall panel was working as he spoke. "Rockwell, Lee, Barnes, and Selsor report to Mr. Kaane."

They found the Cryo in a small wardroom with Commander Brent who greeted them with a small, measured smile.

"We are within some fifty miles of the island chain once designated as Hawaii," said Ury Kaane, "although, as expected, the scanners show only open sea. Commander Brent thinks a series of outsea dives may be of some use, and all four of you are scheduled for this afternoon. I'd suggest the shield suits with tanks until we know more about water conditions from actual entry."

Commander Brent tapped his fingers on the tabletop. His voice was soft. "Rockwell, you'll command the group, of course. But I think what we want more than actual observations and normal analysis is—ha, hmmm—if I might say, is sort of a feel of the sea itself. I may be explaining this badly, but one of the reasons I was persuaded to allow you to join this venture was the simple fact of your youth and the sensitivity to new surroundings which goes with it. I won't care if you come back with a vague report, but I will care if you miss anything, however silly it may seem at the time. Am I clear?"

Toby Lee frowned and unconsciously felt for Kim's arm on the chair beside her.

"Weapons?" asked Kim.

"Laser tubes, I think," said Commander Brent. "Doubt if you find animal life to any degree. We're over the Hawaiian Deep and this part of the ocean is supposed to be pretty much of a sea desert, but what you see report at once. We'll monitor you in all ways. Good luck."

"Monitor us in all ways," mused Tuktu as they suited up in a starboard bubble. "So I'll sing to the boat. When they get an idea of my fine voice I may become a star in one of the entertainment complexes in some great city."

"You know a song called 'Amoeba Though I Am, Nothin' Can Divide Me?'" asked Genright.

"No, but there's a dandy called 'Clam Upon My Knee But Don't Scratch While Climbing,'" said Tuktu.

"A love song?" asked Toby Lee.

"Gets you, eh?"

"Right in the head," snapped Kim. "Let's go."

They popped into the sea at one hundred feet below surface, tested communications and finned away from the hovering submarine. The water was heavy with an unfamiliar density, and Kim reported the fact as he waved the team toward the surface. It was warm too and surprisingly clear. The sunlight above gave them good visibility.

"Seems to be a strong current set," said Toby.

"Stay in the vicinity as best we can," said Kim. "I don't want to get too far away from the boat on this trip."

They surfaced and snapped off their masks in a topside calm as a lake.

"Who's wearing perfume?" asked Tuktu.

"That's air," said Toby. "Old-fashioned kind."

At head-level height there was no horizon, only a merger of green-gray sea with a white sky as they finned in a circle looking along the surface in silence.

Kim felt uneasy although he didn't know why.

"Ho," said Genright. "There's company."

Tuktu's eyes followed the sweep of Genright's upflung arm. Kim and Toby turned in the same direction. Some fifty yards from them were some twenty floating jellyfish masses.

"That's a lot of Portuguese men-of-war in one location," said Kim. "But if we don't mess with them, they won't mess with us."

Toby Lee's voice was small. "I have the funny feeling that something is watching us."

"So do I," added Tuktu soberly.

"Stay on the surface but split up and swim about two hundred yards apart," ordered Kim. "I want to check something."

They did. As they did so the Portuguese men-of-war drifted apart, several moving in the direction of each swimmer.

A small chill rippled down Kim's spine. He snapped back his mask and spoke into his warbler. "Take it down, people, and all the way."

Commanders Brent and Kaane as well as Commander Cassius were waiting for them as they shucked the shield suits and got back into coveralls.

"All right," said Commander Brent as they assembled once again in the small wardroom. "What was that all about? You certainly weren't out long."

"You asked for a report on the unusual," said Kim. "I thought it best to return with it immediately. First, that water out there has an extremely odd feel which in itself isn't too bothersome. All of us have found funny water before in places. But as we surfaced both Toby Lee and Tuktu had the notion that they were being watched. There was nothing up there except a group of jellyfish, the complexes known as Portuguese men-of-war. But when we split into individual swimmers going different directions so did the men-of-war."

"So?" asked Commander Brent frostily.

Ury Kaane snapped his knuckles and nodded.

"So, whether you remember or not, sir," said Kim, "Portuguese men-of-war are plankters, drifters, not swimmers like the nekton. They move with currents or, perhaps, with winds.

"They have no motive power as fish do," continued Kim. "Further, the surface was absolutely calm. There was no breeze. In addition, there was a strong current set which we noticed going up and equally noticeable on the surface.

"Those king-size members of the jellyfish family moved against it. That's all, sir."

"Kim," said the Cryo, "the Portuguese man-of-war is a complex, a composite of animal life. As you know, one animal forms the ballooning float, another makes up the tentacles which gather food, still another digests that

food for the total creature, and a fourth handles the re-
productive process.

"Are you suggesting that this biological mishmash is
suddenly one capable of spying?"

"I thought it best to return and report, sir."

"Hunch, Kim?" asked Commander Cassius softly.

"Yes, sir.

"Gentlemen, I suggest we move another twenty-five
miles west and try another diver team tomorrow," Kim
continued.

Commander Brent shook his head and came to a decision.

"Move," he said. He looked at the young hydronauts.
"You too as well as the boat."

They went back to the men's compartment but Toby
Lee came in as well. She curled on the end of Kim's bunk.

"Monitor us in all ways," said Tuktu. He addressed a
query to the four walls. "Would you think that this tub
had sensing equipment capable of spotting even an invisible diatom? Yes, it does, sir. Yes, sir, it does.

"And how big is a big jellyfish? About the size of a big
barrel, sir. Right, son. And did anybody spot the big
jellyfish? Well, sir, maybe the civilian scientists did. Ah,
ha! But are they speaking to members of the Service?"

"Shut up, Tuktu," said Kim firmly. "Maybe we should
have stayed out later and experimented more."

"No," said Toby Lee. "Just, no."

"What time's dinner?" asked Genright.

"We been bad," said Tuktu inelegantly. "We don't get
none."

Kim looked thoughtful.

The *Polaris* loafed forward.

The divers who left the submarines the next day were crew members, veterans of many Service explorations, and they were casual as they sat through their briefing while Kim, Toby, Genright, and Tuktu listened. They took Kim's description of the Portuguese men-of-war with interest, and the admonitions of Commanders Cassius and Brent about detailed reconnaissance as though they were taking notes on a lecture.

"Use the lasers or the pulsar tubes to test whatever you see," warned Brent, "and make certain that you really see whatever you find. We'll be in the bio-observation room watching you and monitoring."

Tuktu cleared his throat and throttled a small noise.

"We're going up and you'll take off at surface," said Commander Cassius. "Communicate. Speak up at all times. Make no descent greater than two hundred feet, and we'll sink to meet you."

It was Toby Lee who first spotted the jellyfish, again in a gathering of some twenty or thirty forms. "There they are," she said with restrained excitement.

"Don't tell me they moved twenty-five miles since yesterday," snapped Commander Brent. "Not drifting."

"Not necessarily the same group, sir," said Kim.

"Enlarge 'em," ordered Ury Kaane to one of the video control operators. "Let's take a close look."

"Nothing biologically different about them that I can see," said one of the civilian experts.

But as the divers' heads cleared water, the men-of-war separated, clots of them going in different directions.

"That's different," said Ury Kaane.

As he spoke one of the divers reported. "There are the blobs. Shall I tickle one of them?"

"Report on water conditions first," ordered Commander Brent.

"Unusual, sir," interrupted another diver voice. "High temperature, high density, and we seem to be over an upwelling of some sort, a core of even warmer water rising and loaded with nutrients."

"Can't be," said another civilian. "There's twenty thousand feet of sea beneath us, and no upwelling comes that far off a bottom without dispersing."

"I'm tickling," warbled one of the divers, "then we'll go down a hundred and see if anything happens."

Kim could see the diver forms descend, and the boat sunk gently with them.

Suddenly there was a burbling roar in the sound system, a noise like a liquid avalanche, and streaking from somewhere beneath the sub's currently blind side came a school of fish.

It looked like an army of ten-pound bluefish swimming by the thousands, but its units acted like maddened piranhas. It swirled over two divers in a bubbling mass. And, although lasers winked the water into steaming blood, the horrified watchers on the *Polaris* saw the crewmen shredded.

The assault was over in minutes.

"Take it down," said Commander Cassius calmly. He

looked steadily at Kim and spoke once more softly. "Hunch?"

Toby Lee shuddered and grasped Kim's hand. Tuktu and Genright gazed steadily at each other.

There was no time for reflection. The observation screens bloomed with a gigantic figure boiling head on for the bow of the *Polaris.* The boat's speakers brayed. "Whale on collision course! My God, what a whale! It's attacking."

Commander Cassius thumbed a switch.

"Fry it now," he said steadily.

White laser light from a battery of synthetic crystals streamed from the *Polaris.* The oncoming monster shook as it touched its humped head and back. It split wide open into two massive sections and twisted away into the abyss.

"Take her down as ordered," said Commander Cassius.

They held an all-boat conference, all communicators linked, at five thousand feet. Commander Brent impassively demanded a navigational fix and sent a report to the Council of Cities. Then he spoke to the boat, dryly and impassively.

"This is what we know," he said. "We are very close to, and perhaps closer than we think, to the site of the vanished Hawaii burrow city if all the charts from the archives are correct.

"We are under both surveillance and attack.

"That attack involves no mechanical or science weapons.

"It occurred in waters of high temperatures distinguished by warm nutrient-filled upwellings.

"It was made by either self-directed or outer-directed animal life which, while normal forms of sea creatures, act in a completely abnormal fashion.

"I ask speculation, gentlemen, and your best scientific assumptions."

One of the civilian scientists spoke. "I don't agree with your statement of normal forms of sea life. Those fish were completely alien to me. I do not think they were a Pacific species."

Cryo Ury Kaane's violet eyes were somber.

"The clue is biological," he said. "Attack, yes, but with creatures, perhaps, merely trained or conditioned to react. Water conditions? Perhaps abnormal, maybe not for this area."

Kim shifted uneasily in his seat and the motion caught Commander Brent's eye. The coordinator stared at him thoughtfully.

"I am not unaware of your apparently correct action of yesterday, young man," he said. "Were you about to add something to this meeting?"

"Only a wild guess, sir," said Kim. "There is much wider knowledge here than mine."

"Guess then," said Brent.

Instead Kim turned to Toby Lee. "Do you remember what Commander Tod Torrance once told us about the nursery waters at the shark pens?" he asked.

"You're right," she said.

Commander Cassius pointed a finger. "Do you mind sharing what it is you're so right about, Warden?"

"Again, a guess, sir," said Kim. "But Commander Torrance said that a combination of high nutrient, proper saline content, and warm temperatures in sea water formed an exact duplicate of . . ."

Ury Kaane snapped his fingers.

"Amniotic fluid, the same sort that sustains an embryo in its mother's womb, mankind's birth liquid! But spread over so many square miles of sea . . ." His face grew grim. "What sort of a hatch, a birthing would demand sea animal protection unless for another, very special form of sea life, a very precious form of life?"

As Kim watched, Ury Kaane's violet eyes changed to that look he had seen before, that black stare down the corridor of the centuries. The Cryo fainted.

"I can guess," said the imperturbable Commander Brent, his jaw rock muscled and his lips a thin line, "the inhabitants of a sea-covered, pioneer burrow city."

The submarine's medical ESPERS helped the Cryo to his quarters.

Commander Brent closed the meeting.

"I hope all of you experts in your respective fields will consider my assumption seriously, however wild it may be. I remind you that the mission is still Hawaii Search."

He flicked a hand at Kim. "I'll want you to attend a small session later with the Cryo, Commander Cassius, the boat's senior biologist, and myself." He grimaced. "Hunches and guesses. Guesses and hunches, bah!"

"I guess and I hunch," said Tuktu back in their compartment. "Do I get asked to special meetings? No."

"You guess wrong and you hunch up all scroogie," explained Genright.

"I guess right," said Toby Lee pertly, "and I . . ."

"Hunch up mighty pretty," grinned Kim.

"It's because I'm a girl type," she pouted.

"I noticed," said Kim, "but I'm invited because I outrank you all."

Toby Lee patted his cheek. "Order me to do something," she said sweetly.

"Like what?" asked Genright.

"I'd only guess wrong and hunch up all scroogie," beamed Tuktu.

"Well, if I'm going to act smart later, I want a few eyeballs of sack time right now," said Kim suddenly serious.

"Told you I'd guess wrong and hunch scroogie," flipped Tuktu.

"Off I go to find better company and girl talk," said Toby Lee.

The faces in the con chamber were intent as Cryo Ury Kaane talked softly. Commander Brent's was a study in marble.

"The basic assumption is valid," said the Cryo. "When Hawaii burrow was originally stocked, when I left my wife and child there, among the most prominent of its collection for the future were its geneticists. There was Dr. Halver of the New England Institute for Medical

Research, Dr. Hindheimer of California Tech, Dr. Prince from the University of Pennsylvania, and many others.

"All of them had carried on the work begun in evolutionary control started long before them with the discoverers of DNA, the deoxyribonucleic acid which is the main pattern holder in all heredity, and RNA, the ribonucleic acid which is the message-carrying chemical that tells life cells how best to do what DNA determines for them.

"They were masters of what was then called chemical genesis. Simply enough, they were creators of so-called artificial life who could make new humans, if necessary, in a laboratory. Ostensibly they could build a *Homo* superior out of old *Homo sapiens*. . . ."

"Until old homo sap blew the lid off the world," said Commander Cassius softly.

"Exactly, but those men went into the city. I often wondered why," continued the Cryo, "unless it was to continue their work which was to assure some continuity of man stock for a world utterly unsuited to man." His voice was but a whisper. "I also wondered why the selection of Hawaii itself, really only a vast mountain chain subject to volcanic action. Unless," he said, "the planners knew that the scientists of the city would speed their work under the drastic time limits set by both natural and man-made disasters."

"Sir, why did you go Cryo?" asked Kim, then flushed at the impulse which made him interrupt.

"Ask your body-bank specialists and the ESPERS, but

I was a person of promise with an incurable disease at the time. That was long, long ago."

"The Hawaii archives and charts we are now using date back nine centuries," said Commander Brent. "It is possible that the city vanished sometime during the first five of those centuries. The other burrows did not really begin to utilize the sea as we use it now until approximately four centuries ago. It was simply too hot, too radioactive for humans. The cities lived on stock-piled chemicals, synthetic inventions, and forcefully controlled populations.

"But assuming success for any genetic program designed to rebuild humans for indigenous sea life, how many man-stock creatures could be made in one to X-number of years of existence?" asked Brent.

"Comparatively few," answered Commander Cassius.

"Millions," said the senior biologist.

"One of you at a time," snapped Commander Brent.

"With our extensive work in the Service over four hundred years some one or more of our people would have spotted them," said Cassius.

"A moment please," added Ury Kaane. "Knowing a bit about the psychology of men more contemporary to me than any of you, I go along with Commander Cassius. It is possible that the Hawaii city scientists prepared their selected chromosomes and timed them for birth in staggered periods long after their own and their city's death.

"Cybernetics and computer sciences were, perhaps, more advanced than they are today. You in this time lack metals. The men of the past did not. Machines could operate under water, you know, and could be programmed to laboratory tasks as well as to the creation of amniotic environments."

"How about the protective creatures, if that's what they were, as we say today?" asked the senior biologist.

"They too start from cells and could be timed to appear when necessary."

"Sir," asked Kim, "when did the Service first notice unusual occurrences in this area?"

"About two years ago," said Commander Brent.

"I would then guess that in that period there has been two birthings, or hatchings, which have entered the open sea, with every indication that the third is on the way," said the Cryo.

"Would you care to estimate how many of the man-stock sea breed are then in our oceans?" rapped Brent.

"I would not," said Ury Kaane, "but any number will do."

"They are able to reproduce, I assume," said the coordinator.

"I would guess, lavishly."

"Then there will be no third birthing, or hatching, even if we lose this boat and all its hands," said Brent solemnly.

"But why, sir?" burst Kim. "Whatever they are, if they exist at all, they are men and made to keep man alive at a time when their makers thought there could never be a human race at all."

"Good boy," grunted Commander Cassius.

"Not good boy," snapped Brent, "a warden in need of reconditioning." He went on coldly.

"What feeds the hive cities? Answer: the sea. What happens to the cities, all of them, if so-called sentient creatures, thinking creatures in numbers, begin to use the same sea for food, metals, medicines, life itself? What happens when real men, natural men, cannot compete with animals specifically adapted to oceans for their existence?"

"We could ask them to help us," said Kim steadily. "They too are part of man."

"They are not men. But our orders will come from the Council and they will be obeyed."

The Cryo looked at the space around him.

"First find thy rookery," he said, "then ask how to destroy it."

The hydronaut foursome discussed the matter in their own privacy.

"How do we catch these mackerel men? With a hook?" asked Tuktu.

"Mullet men, and you take 'em with a net," drawled Genright.

"Funny, funny," said Kim. "But I don't see the humor."

"We know," said Tuktu.

"It keeps us from crying," said Toby Lee. "And there may be Council members who agree that whatever they are, if they really are, should be saved and made part of all of us."

"I doubt it," said Kim sourly.

The *Polaris* found Hawaii that night, once the largest of a chain of volcanic mountains that stretched from

Midway Island, northwest to east. Sonic topographic scanners measured the peak once known as the Big Island from sea floor to a present height some three hundred feet from the surface. As the *Polaris* cruised easily, radar devices sought out openings in its cliffsides, mapped its physical differences. The boat found peaks upon the giant peak which was the island, many of them named on the old maps: Mauna Loa, Mauna Kea, Kilauea. And it found crater after volcanic crater, all of them now vast, water-filled pipes leading into and, perhaps, through Hawaii to the sea floor.

The *Polaris* cruised around the island and over it. There was a great depression between the two largest peaks, and as the scanners printed facsimile charts, Ury Kaane put his finger on it.

"That's the site of Hawaii city," he said.

Radar, sonar, and occasionally the laser-flash TV cameras picked up strange and sometimes huge animal shapes in the waters about the island. They were not appreciated by any of the divers, although most of the civilian biologists and their technicians enthusiastically advocated capture attempts for study purposes.

The *Polaris* cruised and cruised, unmolested, but with a patience that tried the young wardens.

"What are they going to do, buy it?" asked Tuktu.

Ury Kaane explained. "We are looking for some possible exit vent to the open ocean where the water temperatures are the highest, the nutrient counts the greatest, and where small life could surface immediately without excess pressure strains. Trouble is, it could be a hole five feet in diameter or a big crater itself.

"The technical and biological staffs need time. Besides, I don't think that Commander Brent has orders from the Council as yet." He smiled as he looked at Kim. "Further, I think that some of your remarks upset him slightly. He's a fair and just man, if a cold one."

"How do we get to that hole wherever it is?" asked Genright. "If it's topside at about three hundred feet we could work at that depth in silco suits as well as shields."

"Not without losing divers to that swimming stuff out there," said Tuktu, "and I don't want any white arm like yours. I like my old creamy brown one just fine."

"That white one does get dirtier than most," admitted Genright pensively.

"You could dye it."

"What! A skinny guy like me already."

"Will you two cut it out," snapped Toby Lee.

The Cryo grinned. "I think you'll be using one of the four-man work subs and carrying nerve gas dispensers when we find what we're looking for out there."

"Against whales?" breathed Toby.

"And maybe some thousand-year-old booby traps," said Kim.

"I doubt it," smiled Toby Lee. "Those people wouldn't have left anything that might hurt their own babies."

"Oh, brother," moaned Genright.

"You mean, oh, mother," said Tuktu.

The technicians apparently made their reports and that night Coordinator Commander Brent summoned another all-boat conference using the vessel's communicators. He was sparse with words as usual.

"The first portion of this mission is accomplished. There are two others: explore as fully as possible and destroy this geographical unit of the sea.

"Two four-man work subs will leave their exit bubbles in the morning. They will be armed with gas dispensers and fixed lasers fore and aft, each set with wide-angle beams. One work craft will be manned by crew complement. The other will be staffed by Wardens Rockwell, Selsor, Barnes, and Lee. That crew will explore two sites, each of them tunnels leading into what we believe to be the vanished city itself. The warden crew will explore as far into those vents as possible. The *Polaris* men will stay outside to give whatever protection possible in the event of animal or other hazard.

"Each craft is expected to make a running report. Each will be followed by our instruments. Their own have been set to self-record under maximum sensing capacities—sonic, visual, and physical. The crews will find all visual devices set to 180-degree sweeps."

Commander Brent paused.

"The exploration craft will destroy as fully as possible all life forms found within tunnels, vents, and possible chambers."

Cryo Ury Kaane and Commander Cassius, sitting alongside Kim in the wardroom, were stolid.

"He's the boss, Kim," said Cassius, "and the boss has had his own orders."

"I hope we don't find anything," muttered Kim.

There was a painful twitch at the corners of Ury Kaane's violet eyes. "I don't know why," he said, "but I have the queer feeling that if you do I may not survive the discovery."

Kim was painstaking the next morning. He examined every inch of the eighteen-foot work sub; its A-pack power plant, its compact ballast tanks, its miniaturized instrument board, the view screens, and its weapons. A drop or two of nerve gas, liquid at lethal concentrate, could kill over a wide area of sea, but he made certain that the dispensers were full. He checked the laser, the set, the food locker, and every fitting he could think of to check. He asked for and got a small dip net and a rectangular, screen top box. This he took down the one-man hatch of the work craft himself and stowed.

"Strip," he ordered his crew when they assembled in the discharge bubble.

"Come on, now," said Toby Lee.

"Well, down to bare decency anyhow. I checked with the technicians right after I went over our air tanks. They told me that temperatures over those holes we're about to peek into go as high as the nineties. You know what it will be with four of us in this can."

The *Polaris* crewmen took their craft out of the midship bubble first. Kim followed from the stern launch, adjusting for neutral buoyancy, then setting the automatics to maintain it.

The sea was clear but it boiled with wild life before

the two craft had gone two hundred yards; small fish, sharks of fantastic sizes, other strange creatures—all bent on attacking the small craft.

The lead sub's laser fan winked on and stayed cutting a broad path through the animal concentrate. "Am also using gas," reported Kim's communicator.

"Keep using it," said the steady voice of Commander Cassius from the *Polaris*. "Are you all right, Wardens?"

"Following the lead boat," said Kim, "and all sensing equipment functioning. No use of weapons."

"No music either," muttered Tuktu.

The first site was a funnel-shaped crater some five hundred feet in diameter, and while the *Polaris* crew work sub hovered above it, cruising in a circle around its perimeter, Kim nosed his craft down its slope. It dead-ended in a splintered coral-encrusted vent, and Kim so reported as he maneuvered cautiously for the trip out. "High temperature pocket," he said into the communicator, "pumice and obsidian sides. There is a definite jet forming a sort of separate water column rising from the bottom, but it seems to be coming from a crack in the rock."

"Fine, try the second site, but be careful to spot the boat above you. It is still using weaponry," said Cassius' voice from the *Polaris*.

"We know our friends," interrupted the crew sub. "Come out on the lip at three o'clock, Wardens."

"They should have given this job to a brace of dippy dolphins," griped Genright.

"They found something dippier," said Tuktu with a nervous giggle.

Kim followed the crew boat through a wake of dead and inert carcasses to the second site. He reported as he reached it while the other craft took up its circular station.

"Seems to be a round bore some two hundred feet descending vertically, although it is located on the shoulder of a slope. We'll descend on even keel, plenty room for this canoe. Take a time check on us now."

"And if we ain't back for lunch, mail sandwiches," said Tuktu.

"Share the wealth with us, little brother," said the companion boat. "We'll be right upstairs."

Kim held the boat laterally, operated the tanks manually, and let the craft settle in the middle of the bore. The light from the sea above them vanished into a dot above, and the boat splashed its own illumination upon the walls of a giant shaft.

"I think I'm frightened," murmured Toby Lee.

"Be positive," said Tuktu. "I know I am."

"Shut up and see if one of you can get a spotlight on the walls," ordered Kim.

Genright managed.

Kim spoke into the communicator. "I think we're on it," he said. "Shaft walls look finished, man-made, and smoothed," he reported. "Are you in contact? Are you in contact?"

There was no answer.

At one hundred feet down the shaft, they were still in

blackness. At two hundred, there was a discernible glow, and at two hundred and fifty, the shaft opened into a huge cavern. Kim halted the descent. He tried to raise the *Polaris* and the companion work boat. There was still no contact.

"We're on our own," he said.

And awe-stricken.

Even the irrepressible Tuktu was stunned into shocked silence.

There was light in the giant cavern, a golden illumination that seemed to come from faraway walls. They were suspended in a gold teardrop of vast dimension in the very heart of a mountain.

As Kim moved the work sub forward, the spotlight beam, cutting through the soft radiance and through the clear veil of water, picked up bank after bank of strange machines, of unfamiliar equipment. The sonar devices, indeed all the sonic gear, indicated that many of them were working, if the steady hums and clicks were evidence of function.

Inboard temperature recorders settled at 98.8 degrees Fahrenheit.

The prime source of their mutual shock was in the water itself. It was busy water, alive with bodies by the thousands, child-size forms duplicated over and over again, all of them swimming effortlessly in an endless milling.

They had found the sea babies born of man stock.

Toby Lee giggled hysterically. Tuktu moaned, and Genright clapped both hands to his head as if to dispel a weird dream. Kim merely stared as a man entranced.

"They're cute," whispered Toby, the whisper a near shriek.

Kim shook himself. He strained to make his voice even. "Make sure every recording instrument is functioning," he snapped. "All of you check everything."

The young hydronauts, jarred back to duty, did as he asked.

The sea babies were some two feet in length. Their backs were a pale green-blue from head to tail, and the tail looked like a juncture of ankles with feet turned into a fluke. They looked like dolphins rearranged with their backs less humped and a strange, almost feathery dorsal fin standing alone. Their undersides were a faint, blush-pink. And where pectoral fins should be, there were webbed, translucent fins through which five fingers and an opposite thumb showed clearly, usable fin hands.

Their heads sloped from the back curve into a clearly defined ridge, much as a forehead which then jutted into a long pointed nose. The mouth was a sickle shape like a young moon, and its curve ended in a series of gill slits.

It was the eyes that chilled Kim.

They were round, lidless, completely human with both iris and pupils.

They were violet.

And they radiated intelligence.

It was Tuktu who broke Kim's spell.

"Ten thousand Ury Kaanes equipped to go to sea," he muttered.

"You'll remember the Cryo left a son in the city," mused Toby Lee, "a boy, the boy he thought Kim was, during the quake at the shark pens. It's possible the geneticists used that boy for the original genes, the basic chromosome patterns."

"Too much," said Tuktu somberly. "A father, a Cryo for centuries, returns as grandfather to a whole new human race."

Genright shifted uneasily. He cleared his throat and words stumbled from it.

"What do we use? The nerve gas or the laser beams?"

"You will destroy all life forms as fully as possible," intoned Tuktu.

Toby Lee cried without shame.

They are not men, not natural men, thought Kim, and they will starve the cities, and orders are orders are orders.

A lifetime of psychological and physical conditioning, of discipline and teaching, fought something else in Kim Rockwell, Warden II on special Rover duty. And lost!

"There will be no weapon used under my command," he said slowly. "But I will record any protest from any of you for future hearings. I urge you to think hard. Your careers are at stake; perhaps, under strict Service rules, your lives."

"Pishy-tushy, tootie," said Genright.

"Hear the hard captain," grunted Tuktu.

Toby Lee flung herself forward and kissed Kim through a blur of her own tears.

"You could keep your knee out of my neck," snapped Genright.

"Look," said Kim uncomfortably, "while we still have jobs we're working. First, how long have we been in this hole?"

"Three-quarters of an hour," answered Tuktu.

"They'll give us more time than that topside," said Kim. "Listen, I brought a box, just in case. It will hold two of these little . . ."

"Brothers," said Genright.

"But I want a girl and a boy," grinned Kim. "And hot as it is in here, I'm going to a pound or two over sea pressure on the bottom hatch. Toby can pop out with the net and pick up a pair. We'll fill the box with this amniotic water and take 'em home with us."

"You sure Toby knows the difference between boys and girls?" asked Tuktu loftily.

"Boys hunch up all scroogie," said Toby.

"Tank and shield suit at this depth," said Kim, "no matter who you kick getting into it."

They watched the capture which was no capture at all. The net was unnecessary. As Toby slid into screen view, she was surrounded by the sea babies.

"You'd think they wanted to cuddle," muttered Tuktu.

The work sub was three-quarters of the way up the exit bore when the boat broke into a babble of sound.

"Come in, Rockwell. Come in. Come in. Report."

The companion sub and the *Polaris* were each talking.

"This is Rockwell," said Kim steadily. "Cavern in the mountain is an actual laboratory, and functioning. Found rookery. Repeat, found incubator. Am homeward bound. Will follow lead boat. Any instructions?"

There was a long moment of silence. Then clear, distinct, and level, Coordinator Commander Brent's voice filled the small craft.

"Rockwell, did you carry out your mission?"

As if by some unspoken rehearsal, Toby Lee, Genright, and Tuktu held up their right hands with crossed fingers.

"Part of it," said Kim quietly. "We found the life forms, and they are man-stock sea babies."

There was no way to describe Commander Brent's returning voice.

"Sea babies? Sea babies?" it said, the steady tone sliding up the scale. "Did you or did you not destroy?"

"Not a one," replied Kim.

There was a garble. The commander's voice seemed to be fighting a way through a swamp of algae jell.

"Repeat, sir. Repeat," said Kim.

Commander Cassius' robust tones filled the work boat.

"The man said, 'thank God, Rockwell.' Now all of you get home. Stop use of nerve gas. Repeat, stop all use of nerve gas. Use only lasers if necessary. Home now. That is all."

The wardens stared at each other.

"What's he mean, the man said thank God?" asked Genright.

"We're just too valuable to shoot," said Tuktu.

Kim could feel that mystic sense of Toby Lee enter

his mind, that always warm and surprising closeness. She said it for him.

"The Council of Cities changed its mind," she guessed.

"I don't think I can take much more of today," griped Genright.

"You better set yourself then," said Tuktu. "I've got that old bell in my ears telling me that there's more to come."

There was.

When the work subs were stowed back in their portion of the pressure bubbles aboard the *Polaris*, and the wardens were once again in coveralls and ready for open ship interrogation by both commanders as well as the technicians assigned by Brent to the routine, Kim off-loaded his specimen box, a small tarpaulin over its top. Tuktu and Genright carried it to the biological section of the *Polaris* with Brent, Cassius, and Ury Kaane at their heels.

They placed the box on a long metal table, and Kim removed its cover.

The sea babies rolled and sloshed in their watery cradle. There was a stunned silence in the room. The small creatures lifted their heads toward the ceiling lights.

Their wide, round violet eyes stared into the round, wide voilet eyes of Ury Kaane.

The Cryo went mad.

He stretched an agonized hand toward the box and

froze into a forever darkness as deep as the one in which he had been placed when Hawaii city was born.

The medical ESPERS took him away.

The Council of Cities had indeed changed its mind, explained Commander Brent to Kim and his companions sometime later as they sat in the con section of the *Polaris* with Commander Cassius. He was brittle, trying to bend as he spoke.

"My superiors reasoned what you, Rockwell, apparently knew by instinct. Namely, that your sea babies were man stock and designed by loyal, earth patriots trying, with God's help, to make sure some form of mankind would endure. I take some comfort in the fact that the Council's original order reflected my own thinking, in short, that the man-like cities could starve if creatures designed for the sea were permitted, with man's intelligence, to exploit the sea.

"I think I take more comfort in the fact that some of the Council, all cold men, raised the question of murder at a time soon to come when this blasted planet would heal enough to demand all of the man stock possible to obtain—any color, shape, form, and type of it.

"I am not used to explaining things to children, especially young wardens whose ideas of discipline vary from my own, but I also think that there were members of the Council who decided that they would eat better if more skilled practitioners of life in the sea than those not designed for it were busy about the business of supplying the needs of the cities.

"This, of course, may ultimately put the Service out of work."

Commander Cassius interrupted softly.

"It may be," he said. "I think the Service, however, will demand a new type of Rover for some time. There will be the work of locating the dispersed—oh, ah—oceanic men fish, fish-men, making them friends, if possible, establishing mutual bonds of need, enlisting their help in the tasks of the future.

"If so," he continued, "I shall make my recommendations for candidates for such Rover duty, and they will include those of you in this room."

The wardens knew when to keep silence. They did so.

Coordinator Commander Brent spluttered.

"You can't run a Service on hunches and guesses, sir. Guesses and hunches, hunches and guesses!" He stared at Kim, and his face broke into a startling grin. "But I shall add my own recommendations."

The *Polaris* stayed in the area. For days its experts made the dive down the bore to the incubator cavern, examining the machines, the details of the laboratory built centuries ago, searching for records, delving always for more knowledge of the original city. Hawaii hive had been long gone, its original life snuffed out. What remained swam placidly in the nutrient nursery.

The *Polaris* stayed in the area. It made sure that the toxic nerve gas waters were diluted by winds, currents, and dissolved into harmless solution.

Still, the *Polaris* stayed in the area.

Then one morning as the sun stained the eastern rim of the heaving Pacific, and the shreds of surface mists colored with new light into cloud-patch confetti, the *Polaris* watched an exodus.

Thousands of tiny forms bobbed to the top of the sea and the new sun winked into violet eyes. Thousands of small, proud dorsal fins feathered the wave foam, and thousands of flukes churned those forms into directed motion.

The school headed north as the *Polaris* tracked it and recorded its passing. Every view screen on the submarine was in action.

Kim, Toby Lee, Genright, and Tuktu sat in the small wardroom and watched, mutually embraced in their own silence.

"Guesses and hunches. Hunches and guesses," said Tuktu. "You can't run a Service on guesses and hunches. But it's my guess and my hunch that we'll see them again."

"Scroogie," said Genright flatly.

"Want to go back to the lab?" asked Toby Lee. "It's time to feed the babies."

A familiar name to many magazine readers, Carl L. Biemiller has been a journalist most of his life, as assistant publisher for the Camden *Courier-Post* and the Philadelphia *Daily News,* and as executive editor of *Holiday* magazine. He is currently the editorial director of Bell and Stanton, a prominent New York public relations firm.

He lives on the shore line of New Jersey where he, as he writes, "turned on with oceans many years ago." He is married and has four grown sons.